THE VAMPIRE IN FREE FALL

At the last possible moment I swerved violently to the right, just making it onto the exit ramp. The patrol car was large and powerful, but it simply couldn't corner like the Porsche, and it blazed off down the freeway, out of the game. But the Russians had time to adjust, and they followed me up the ramp.

I careened right at Lincoln and hurtled along the street. We weren't far from Jager's office, but I had no intention of going there. Instead I sped north. I was beginning to realize that these guys weren't going to get lost. So I decided it was time to be a vampire . . .

THE VAMPIRE IN FREE FALL

D1707314

the

VAMPIRE

in

FREE FALL

Jim Hull

CreateSpace
Scotts Valley, CA
2010

KATHI –
TANX 4 B-ING A
TINKER FAN!

The Vampire in Free Fall

Published by CreateSpace, Scotts Valley, CA

Registered: Writers Guild of America West

ISBN: 1450577245

EAN-13: 9781450577243

THE VAMPIRE IN FREE FALL

PROLOGUE

They say monsters differ from humans in three ways: they are immortal; they are immensely strong; and they never travel beyond Earth.

By monsters, I mean vampires. Other creatures – werewolves, ghouls, yeti, windigos – can be classified as monstrous, but most of what I know involves vampires, so I'll limit myself to them.

Of course, almost nobody believes in vampires anymore. By now, in the twenty-third century, the light of science has long since poked into the dark corners of human fears, dispelling the fog of superstition. Still, there always remain a few true believers who insist that night-stalking, blood-drinking creatures are real. They argue endlessly among themselves about how vampires differ from humans. The debate is a moot one between diehards, and slightly pathetic.

But let's play *What-If*. The first two differences make good sense. Humans today have conquered aging and disease, but they get into accidents, shoot each other, and drive drunk off bridges. The result? Their life expectancy averages about three hundred years – a poor excuse for immortality. Vampires, on the other hand, are supposed to be dead, which would make them kind of hard to kill; in theory, at least, they could go on forever. Meanwhile, humans have invented power suits that let them jump over buildings, lift up cars, bend steel, and so on. Naked, though, they'd be no match – in strength, speed, or cunning – for a vampire.

Now, what about that third trait, involving space travel? Those who believe in vampires assume they wouldn't venture beyond the protection of Earth's shadow: solar radiation in the vacuum of space surely would fry them to ash. But you could argue just as easily that most spaceships are well shielded against the parts of sunlight that harm vampires. What's more, at distances beyond Jupiter, even the most sensitive of them would barely get a tan.

3

This idea, then – that these creatures cannot, or will not, travel into space – is merely a quibble among fanatics. Meanwhile, the very notion of vampires seems, in our rational age, sort of quaint.

It's strange how, in a crisis, odd thoughts will pop into one's head. These musings on the nature of vampires flitted idly through my mind as I stood at the sink in my stateroom aboard a luxury space liner on its return from the moons of Saturn, staring down at the ashy remains of my left hand – its fingers already crumbled off, the searing burn of the wound's remorseless, slow advance edging up toward my wrist like a gangrene of the undead – and reached for a butcher knife I'd stolen from the ship's galley.

You see, I *am* a vampire. I'm one of those monsters nobody believes in. But if I didn't remove this infection quickly, I would be destroyed.

And so I began to saw away at my own arm.

PART 1

IN COUNTRY

1

There is one thing every vampire can claim: "I wasn't always like this." My death and conversion took place when I was in my twenties, separated from my patrol in a dank, leech-infested jungle in Southeast Asia on Earth. It happened fast. One moment I was a soldier, worried about finding my squad, concerned over what I was going to do with my life after I mustered out, and wondering whether I would score a cute little Saigon sweetie when our three-day leave came up at the end of the month. The next moment I was dead. And very upset about it.

I've always been curious about the world, my interests wide ranging. In fact, I'm a bit of a knowledge hound. I did well in high school, my head in books while other kids played football or ran for student council or took drugs or goofed off. At the university, I chafed at the slow, stiff world of academe, and in a foolish protest I stopped attending classes or doing coursework. Of course I flunked out. If that weren't enough, I then received a low draft number. And so it came to pass that I was inducted into the armed services. I advanced to Army Spec-4 and found myself up-country in that ridiculous war between my homeland, the old United States of America, and a tiny, crowded, unimportant little strip of tropical trouble called Vietnam (which you will recognize today, over two hundred years later, as a southern coastal province of the Chinese Protectorate).

Our squad leader was a staff sergeant. Naturally we called him Sarge. He could be tough and nasty, but most of the time Sarge had the easygoing amiability of someone who had seen everything and didn't much care anymore. He would go on about how screwed up the war was, but when we came under fire he was all business. Quietly we admired him. To this day, though, I can't remember his real name.

We were scouting a jungle region near the narrow center of the country, searching for signs of recent enemy activity. The North Vietnamese troops were fairly good at staying out of our sights. Their elite fighters, the Vietcong, had commando training and could evade most detection. Our job was to find signs of either – and, should we encounter them, engage them in battle.

We were resting, hunkered down out of sight at the edge of a vine-tangled glade, grabbing a quick bite to eat. Sarge crawled over to me and whispered, "I want you to scout the trail ahead for traps and spikes. Take your time, there's no rush. Stay down, give it about ten minutes in one direction, then come back. Got it?"

I groaned. I had the best eyes in the squad for this sort of thing, so I had to do it the most. Scouting was nerve-wracking, exacting work, and there was no guarantee that you would complete the task unscathed. "Okay, Sarge," I mumbled, grabbed my M14 rifle, re-slung my backpack, and slipped out of cover.

I moved slowly and methodically down the trail. The sun, very low in the west, filtered glumly through the thick foliage; visibility wasn't the best. Straining to see, poking my bayonet into bushes to check for traps and spikes, I didn't notice that the path had forked behind me. After about ten minutes of recon, I turned back, only to discover I didn't know which path to take. I made a guess, kept moving, and stepped into a stream that hadn't been there before. I back-tracked, but soon I was hopelessly lost.

I had no radio. In these situations you didn't exactly stand up and shout, "Where are you guys?!" That would merely bring enemy fire onto your position.

Exhausted, cut off from my squad, I sat under a palm tree just after sunset and reached down to pull a leech off my calf. Beyond my boots I saw the black slippers of a Vietcong who hadn't been standing there a second earlier. Stunned at being caught off guard, I grabbed for my firearm, but the Asian made a blurred motion and the rifle disappeared. I heard a crunch as it landed in a bush dozens of yards away. The little man in black pajamas had reached down, picked it up, and hurled it with tremendous force, all in the span of a finger snap. I stared up at him in sudden terror. He gazed down at me and smiled. I saw the glint of very long incisors.

Before I could take all this in, the enemy soldier yanked me to my feet and grabbed me by the shoulders. I squirmed but couldn't move in his iron grip. Holding me, he took a few steps, and I saw the jungle whirl past. We stopped in a clearing I didn't recognize. Smiling again, he uttered a few words in Vietnamese. I recognized "hungry" and "desire" – did he need food?

Then his mouth was at my throat, and a flash of pain coursed through me. My arms and legs felt as if they were shriveling. I felt faint, the light fading from my eyes as if the twilight had turned suddenly to darkest night. I tried to scream, but all I could do was grunt.

None of this made any sense. Maybe I was dreaming. I willed myself to wake up. But the pain continued, flooding me. My pulse fibrillated. I wondered, "Am I having a heart attack?" In the midst of all this, I thought idly, *This guy is the biggest leech I've ever seen.*

Abruptly he stopped his ghastly feeding. Cradling my weakened form in his arms, he bit down on his own wrist. Blood bubbled up from the wound. He turned to me and spoke stridently in Vietnamese. I recognized the word "Drink!" Something deep within me demanded that I put my mouth on his wrist. I obliged.

The taste of his blood was exhilarating! I sucked hard, my thirst a primitive craving. I heard him say the regional words for "Good, very good."

I fell back, sated. At once my body began to shake and quiver. New pain lanced through me. I lay on the ground, twisting in agony. Minutes turned into hours, but the extreme pain continued. I wondered if I had finally gone to Hell.

The little man, who had so viciously sucked the life out of me, now stood guard. He watched my progress as pain flooded through me like a river, surging in waves along my insides to the very tips of my fingers and toes.

I had once, years earlier, experienced a brief, acute case of juvenile gout. I had come to think of that pain as the most anyone could bear. Now it felt as if I had suffered a massive attack of gout in every inch of my body. There is no other way to describe how horrible that feeling was. To this day, despite who I have become, I don't wish it upon anybody.

Except, perhaps, my chosen enemies. But we'll get to them later.

2

As the night advanced, I slipped in and out of consciousness. From time to time my fevered brain heard – or thought it heard – sounds I recognized, the voices of my squad. Were they searching for me?

By the time dawn approached, the pain had ebbed. I tried to sit up. But the little Vietnamese man pushed me back down. I was too weak to fight him. He began digging furiously in the damp ground. When he had excavated a hole the size of a tall, blond American soldier, he dumped me unceremoniously into it. Before I could raise an arm to protest, he filled it in, burying me beneath several feet of earth. The panic that gripped me was as terrible as the pain I had felt during the night. I fought desperately to escape, but the little man sat on the mound and held it in place. I clawed my way toward the surface, but each handful only caused more dirt to fall into its place. A horrible panic of claustrophobia overcame me and, pressed down by the heavy earth, I screamed and screamed. Dirt entered my lungs and I coughed and gagged, the terror relentless.

Finally, panic-stricken but too spent to struggle further, I grew still. I gulped down my fright and wondered what would happen next.

Weirdly, I felt overpowered by sleepiness. Despite a storm of fear and pain, I gave in to the deeply enticing drowsiness and quickly fell asleep.

I suffered horrible dreams of having the blood sucked out of me, of being buried alive. A part of me – the part that now and then could cancel a particularly awful nightmare and wake me – wanted to do so now. But somehow I knew the dreams and my recent waking moments were so similar that there was no point in choosing between them. My body craved the sleep, and so I slept.

I was awakened by a sudden onrush of air against my face. I opened my eyes to see the little man digging away at

10

the same earth with which he had buried me. Terrified of him, I yelled and shrank back. But he smiled that eerie smile of his, and somehow my fright ebbed. Slowly, ponderously, I sat up and peered over the edge of the hole. It was night.

The little man squatted down next to my informal grave and, staring fiercely at me, began to speak. He uttered words in Vietnamese, of which I'd only learned the basics. Strangely, though, I understood him perfectly.

"You are dead now," he began. "You will be thirsty, but not for water. You will desire the blood of humans."

"Dead? What do you mean?" I demanded hoarsely. I coughed up some dirt.

"You will understand in time. Now you will thirst, and you must quench that thirst."

I stared back at him. This was impossible. This whole situation was beyond reason.

He leaned in. "But you must *never* drink from my people! You may taste only of your own kind."

"Americans?" I whispered.

"Americans only. No Vietnamese. If you drink from my people, I will know, and I will find you. And punish you."

I had no idea what he meant by all this. I struggled to stand, but he put a hand on my shoulder.

"You must be careful!" he warned. "You must be cautious. You are different now. Your comrades believe you are dead. Let them think that. It will keep you safe and give you freedom."

I stared at him. "What did you do to me? What right do you have to—"

He laughed. "*Right*? In war? When you Americans come here to kill us? Instead, I have given you a gift. Thank me, and use it well."

"Use it? Use what? *For* what?"

"You will see. Follow your instincts and you will find the right path." He paused. "But you must never move about in the daytime. The sun's light will hurt you."

He made it sound like I was a vampire or something. I stood and reached for the edge of the hole, intending to muscle up onto the ground above. Instead, I fairly leapt through the air. I landed, stumbling, about twenty feet away.

Astounded, I looked back at him. He smiled, and suddenly he jumped to the top of a palm tree above us. Hanging from its fronds, he reached down and patted the side of the palm trunk just beneath him. "Jump to here!" he called.

I stared up at him. *Right*, I thought. Yet moments earlier I had jumped farther than ever – by a long way. On impulse, I squatted and sprung upward. I sailed clear over the top of the palm, yelling with fright, to crash down on the bushes beyond. Sharp pains coursed through me as I struggled to stand. I looked down and saw that I had broken my left shin, the bone making an ugly dogleg. Yet, as I watched, it straightened itself, painfully. Just as quickly the pain was gone. I pulled up my trouser leg and saw a heavy, dark bruise on my calf that faded even as I watched.

It was then I realized I had landed on one of the bamboo spears fashioned by the North Vietnamese to skewer unsuspecting American soldiers. They were usually tipped with a deadly nerve poison and hidden near jungle pathways. This one had gone clean through my left buttocks and halfway into my right cheek. I cried out, "Oh crap! I'm a goner!" I yanked at the shaft and it slipped out of my body, the pain causing me to gasp. But the wound healed almost instantly; in moments it had disappeared. I waited for the nerve poison to work its way into me, expecting the shivers and nausea that foretold death. But none came.

Dazed, disbelieving, I walked slowly back to the palm tree and looked up. But the little Vietnamese man with the long teeth had disappeared. I looked around the clearing. There was no trace of him, except for the hole in the ground where I had been buried during the day, and the mound of dirt next to it.

I was alone. I was, the little man had told me, dead. I had a lot to think about.

And I was thirsty.

3

For three months, I was wild with my new powers. I felt as if I could run faster than a cheetah, even if the jungle offered few open straightaways. I could jump high enough to reach the tops of tall trees. I could leap clear across rice paddies. My hearing was now intensely acute: I heard the sounds of animals slinking through the undergrowth a quarter mile away. My vision was pinpoint sharp, as if I had suddenly received miniature telescopic implants in my eyes. I could see tiny details hundreds of feet away – a lovely flower, an insect crawling on a log, a spider weaving a web. I traveled during the quiet and dark of night, yet it felt as if it were still the bustling daytime.

My strength was enormous. Once, when walking backward and gazing up at some animals in the high canopy, I bumped my head against a palm tree behind me. For a moment I felt an irrational flash of anger. I whirled, pulled the palm straight up out of the ground, and hurled it like a javelin into the forest. It crashed into some trees, knocking one down.

Oddest, though, were the voices. All around me I could hear people talking. At first I thought I was wandering through a crowded part of the jungle. But soon I realized that these voices were the conversations of people miles away. Many were American soldiers on patrol, and from their overheard conversations I found I could keep up with the war's progress, along with news from America and the rest of the world. Stranger still, I could understand the Vietnamese, both soldiers and locals. I thought they were speaking English, but before long I knew that something had quickened in my mind, so that I could figure out their words fast enough to keep up with the conversations. Too, I began to suspect that I had gained the ability to read minds. Sometimes I didn't hear words at all, yet I had the sense that someone had spoken, their thoughts translating themselves into talk in my head.

And of course there was the thirst. Always the thirst.

I felt compelled to be near humans. Some craving drove me to search for them. With my vastly increased power, speed, and acuity, I had no trouble tracking them down, Americans or Vietnamese. I remembered the little man's warning and focused on the Yanks. When I found them, I would hide in the trees and look down at them. Even fifty yards away, I could make out every word of their conversations. When the wind was right, I could smell them. Smell their blood.

If you were starving and the odor of a cooked meal wafted past your nose, you'd know a small fraction of the violence of my reaction to the smell of human blood. Sweet and sour, redolent and complex like a fine wine, the blood coursing through the soldiers' veins excited and enticed me. It sang a Siren song, drawing me unstoppably into the fate that quickly became my life. I wanted to taste their blood, to touch it, to swim in it. And, most of all, I lusted to drink it, to suck great draughts of the dark-red liquid down into myself.

And so I began to feed on the young soldiers.

American war casualties mounted during that time. Many men went missing; others were found with their throats slashed, some with limbs or heads gone. The officer staff, bureaucratically cautious and incurious, simply chalked it up to improved tactics by the Vietcong. I was considered MIA, and it never occurred to anyone that the newly dead and missing were victims of a *vampire*. This gave me free rein, and I made the most of it.

A typical night would begin as I clawed my way up from the dank tomb of a hole in which I'd buried myself that morning. Dirty and disheveled – and, after a few weeks, naked, as the thorns and branches of the jungle slowly ripped my Army fatigues to shreds – I would skulk through the jungles and paddies of central Vietnam in search of American troops. When I found, say, a patrol on bivouac, I would wait for hours until the men were asleep, then quickly and silently crawl up from behind and grab the man on watch, yanking him back into the darkness, where I would drank from his neck, one filthy hand clamped over his mouth to

14

prevent his screams from alerting the others.

At first I was so ravenous that I would return to a given camp and make away with a second soldier, pulling him from his sleeping place and, within seconds, devouring the scarlet life force within him. If that weren't enough to slake my desire, I'd go back to take a third meal.

Each time, the taste of blood was so delicious, so exquisite, so enticing that I would suck all the harder on the victim's neck, to pull every ounce of sweet, bloody nectar from his body. After a couple of weeks I realized I was leaving a trail of dead bodies totally drained of blood. This seemed like poor tactics. Eventually even the most hardened cynic among the soldiers would begin to suspect that something beyond mere enemy action was taking place. I learned to drink more calmly, stopping when I had consumed less than half a man's blood volume. It helped that, as time passed, my raging urges subsided, and I found I didn't need as much as I had during the first few weeks of my new existence.

In this way, I learned a bit of discipline – a trait that would save me many times in the months and years to come.

Sometimes I would drape the bodies over the little bamboo spears set up by the Communists, pressing them down until the spears pierced into them to create a false impression as to cause of death. At other times I might simply rip their heads from their torsos, drop the larger remains, and carry the head a mile or two away, to bury it where it might never be found.

Perversely, on more than one occasion I would hold onto a head for the entire evening, bringing it down into the earth with me when it was time for sleep. I found myself murmuring to these heads as I lay underground, buried beneath mounds of dirt, telling them about my adventures. Later I realized this was my way of cooling the loneliness that had begun to boil up inside me.

My conscience gurgled up, too, from time to time, making me wonder why I had abandoned my countrymen in so ghoulish a fashion. The answer, of course, was that I was no longer one of them. From acquaintances, they had become prey; from fellow soldiers, they had turned into objects of my hunt. Most of this, however, was lost on me as I reveled in my freakish new life, living merely to slake the thirst.

I never again heard or saw my old squad. Finally I assumed they had been reassigned to some other part of the country. This was just as well: they had so recently been my companions, but I wasn't entirely sure, had I run into them, that I wouldn't have fed off them.

At no time, though, did I ever try to kill a Vietnamese. Even Americans of Asian descent I avoided. The terror of that horrible night with the little Vietcong vampire would flood back over me if I were merely to see a South Vietnamese villager. The little man's words had been clear: I was to take only American blood. The thought that he might find and hurt or destroy me, should I disobey him, kept me nicely in check.

One dawn, I tried an experiment: I stuck my hand up through the dirt of my improvised sleeping grave, to see what would happen when sunlight broke through the thick trees and touched my skin. At the time, I half knew it was a foolish thing to do, since it was a game I couldn't afford to lose. But curiosity had gotten the better of me, and I had rarely been one to squirm at danger when I might learn something interesting. I was so sleepy, though, that I dozed with my hand still above ground. A sharp, burning pain woke me. I yanked my arm back down into the crypt. The hand felt as if it had been singed on a stove. But the pain subsided quickly; I fell back to sleep. That evening, as I clambered up out of my hole, I remembered the hand. Glancing down at it, I saw that the skin on one side was darkened and reddish, as if it had gotten an all-day sunburn. I had no idea how long it had been exposed to the sun, so I didn't learn much from my experiment – except that the light hadn't killed me outright. But that in itself was interesting.

Sometimes, sated from a kill and wandering late in the evening, I would approach a small village, where I'd climb a tree or squat down in the bushes and listen to the voices as they spoke of the day's events – of the kid who had broken his foot, or the chicken coop that had lost a gate hinge and released the flock, or the American soldiers who had passed through, dropping off a box of candy bars as a gift. The sounds of the voices and the murmurs of the peoples' thoughts soothed me. I began to look forward to these nighttime visits, as if they were radio programs and I was back at home in America, rapt in childlike attention after a warm meal.

I began to notice snippets of talk about someone the villagers called "The Good Demon" – a man, dressed in Vietcong mufti, with superhuman powers who protected the villages in conflict zones by killing the soldiers from the south, drinking their blood, and leaving the bodies for the villagers to pilfer and mutilate. The voices I heard spoke of this godlike man with awe and fear and respect. It wasn't long before I knew they were speaking of the same little man who had given me the dark gifts I now possessed. I wondered if my own kills had been credited to him by the villagers. I suffered a bit of wounded pride at the thought.

Was he using me to increase his fame with the locals, the way an artist takes credit for his apprentice's work? That seemed like an odd motive. I turned it over and over in my head but couldn't come up with a satisfying reason for my current existence. *Why did he do this to me? Why not just kill me?*

4

Eventually my loneliness got the better of my hunger. Eating them was one thing – I had gotten used to the idea of humans as dinner – but simply being around people was a pleasure that, strangely, I missed. I decided to make contact with them.

I had no intention of returning to the Army, where I would be court-martialed for desertion – and, should they figure out what I had become, executed. Perhaps they would tie me to a post to smolder, screaming, as my body turned to ash, or whatever vampire bodies did in the sun. On the other hand, the best chance of meeting people, while at the same time hiding among them from the military police, would be in the teeming southern capital, Saigon.

I traveled by night on foot. I avoided the exposed rice paddies and villages, making my way at a good clip through the thick, entangling jungle, where I could stay hidden from most eyes. I stopped once, late on the first night, to eat and discard a single American soldier who happened to be sleeping well off to one side of his platoon's encampment. By midnight of the second day I reached the bright, bustling city.

The sensations were intense. The lights shone with colorful brilliance. The noises seemed almost to grab and shake me. The smells especially were strong, much stronger than I had remembered. The odors of cooking, of car and scooter exhaust, of the people themselves, were way beyond redolent as they hung limply on the humid air. It puzzled me, how intense everything felt. Then I remembered: the last time here, I had been a human soldier. Now I was different. Without trying, I could feel much more than in the past. The city had seemed noisy and congested before; now it was off the scale. This would take getting used to.

Even more than the sensations were the voices. I could hear thousands of conversations at once, a cacophony that threatened to unhinge me. I found, though, that they would fade into the background when I focused on any one item of interest: a colorful sign, a lovely garden, a beautiful woman. The voices quickly became a sort of hissing in my ears, a tinnitus I could ignore.

At first I had no trouble moving through the dark side streets, unseen – despite my pale skin – due to the great speed I could muster. I moved almost instantly down alleyways or through backyards, past hanging laundry and chicken coops and prostitutes. Exhilarated, I ran naked along the lanes, now and then for fun clanging noisily on corrugated rooftops as I jumped from building to building. I indulged my powers, amused that my speed made me invisible to the humans I passed.

Then I hit a power line.

Saigon was cobwebbed with telephone, electric, and guy-wires. I noticed them right away, but in the gloom they were hard to see, even with my vampiric eyes. In my joy at rediscovering the sights and sounds of Saigon with my newly heightened senses, I grew careless.

It was a simple beginner's mistake. As a new vampire, I had grown cocky, the way a motorcyclist with a few hundred miles under his belt starts to take risks, overreaches, and goes down. I had gotten lazy about checking where I was headed, and while hurdling a rooftop – looking off to the side, my eyes attracted by a nearby street crowd – the power line clipped me in the neck.

The force snapped my vertebrae. Distinctly I heard the crack. The pain stabbed me like a knife. The line separated, whipped around, and struck me as I fell off the roof. Thousands of volts arced through me; the impact was so great, I blacked out.

The next thing I remembered was lying in a darkened yard, a dog sniffing at my face and then backing away, growling. I tried to sit up but couldn't work my limbs. My neck hurt like hell. As I lay there, dazed, I could feel a painful shifting and a sudden warmth in my neck. Then my feet and arms worked again, and I sat up. Apparently my body had healed itself almost instantly. (A century later, I would chat with a human who reported the same sensations when nanobots repaired his broken back.)

The backyard seemed especially dim, and for a moment I worried that my eyes had been damaged. Woozy, I managed to tumble over a fence. I found myself on a street where every house seemed coated in pitch. Then I realized my encounter with the power line must have cut electricity to the neighborhood. The thought made me laugh. Barely in town an hour, and already the vampire had caused trouble.

Chastened, I slowed my pace to a trot. I skirted the wide main avenues of the capital and searched instead for the crowded, crammed places I'd known from weekends on military leave. I jumped up onto the tiled roof of an old building and looked down on a street filled with late-night shoppers, drunken revelers, hookers, and people on errands for God knows what purpose. Even after midnight, the street swam with bicycles and motor scooters and cars.

A few buildings down, I noticed a booth filled with cheap American clothes. With the speed of a bird flitting through the streets, I leapt down and dashed across the avenue to the booth, where I promptly stole a pair of jeans, a t-shirt, and a pair of sandals while the vendor stood outside, smoking a cigarette.

From there I moved quickly through the bright city night until I found an old French Colonial office building. I located a side door, twisted the knob and broke its lock, and snuck inside. Down a dark hallway I glided until I found a bathroom. I used a sink to clean off the grime of jungle life. Then I donned the first clothes I'd worn in a couple of months. I looked in the mirror.

I was stunned. The face that stared back was mine, yet hauntingly different. The skin was icy pale; the blue eyes burned with a glow, as if heated from within. But something even more startling confronted me. When human, I had thought of myself as okay looking, but now my face had become handsome, almost beautiful. My dark-blond hair was still a bit long for Army regulation; the three days of stubble I had on my cheeks when I'd gotten lost on patrol was still there, as if no time had passed.

I looked down at the cheap pants I'd pilfered. They were too short. Also, the shirt was a bit tight. I would need to improve my duds before long.

I remembered a doorway I had passed in the hall. I walked back to it. Painted on the glazed window in the top half of the door was the French word *"Bibliotheque"*. I opened the door and stepped into the library. The room was dark, but my reborn eyes could pick out details better than infrared scopes. Quickly I found my way to a tall shelf that held two encyclopedias, one in French and one in English. I turned to the English one, found the volume for "V", and flicked through the pages to the article titled "Vampire".

I was surprised to find that I could read much more quickly than in the past – the few pages flew by and I was finished in seconds. I learned that vampires were thought of as fictional; that convention held that they were dead, yet animated; that they could be destroyed by sunlight, decapitation, fire, a stake through the heart, bullets made of silver, and, sometimes, by starvation when human blood was scarce.

I resolved to remember these possible dangers in the days and weeks ahead. After all, I mused, there *is* truth in fiction.

5

By the time I stepped back out onto the Saigon streets, the vivid and lively atmosphere of the great city had ebbed. A clock on a wall showed it was past three a.m., and as I walked I could see that most of the clubs and bars were empty of patrons or closed. It might be better if I waited till early tomorrow evening to make my first try at meeting people, when there'd be more to choose from.

I noticed I'd begun to feel the ache of blood hunger. I kept an eye out for Americans. Before long I noticed a knot of them, well into their cups and singing a rock-n-roll song popular on Armed Forces Radio. I backed into the shadows and waited until they moved off, and of course one of them was slower than the rest. He was a young man still in his teens. As the rest of them rounded a corner, I grabbed him, dragged him into an alleyway, and made short work of him. His blood tasted strange. It occurred to me that the alcohol in his system was affecting my taste buds.

I pulled my head back and watched him die. He looked up at me, his face slackening as his life slipped away. And then he whispered, "Why?"

My jaw dropped in surprise. Blood dribbled down my chin. I wanted to ask, "What did you say?" But his eyes were glazed; he was already gone.

I dropped his body, backed away, then turned and ran.

I didn't stop running until I had found the old French Colonial building. Quickly re-entering, I hurried down corridors until I found a stairway to the basement. There, in a darkened storeroom that looked like it hadn't been used in years, I found an old wooden crate, picked it up with two fingers, and carried it to the darkest corner of the room. I laid it against the wall, climbed inside, and pulled the lid down over me.

My eyes stared into the pitch blackness. "Why?" my young victim had asked. Why, indeed.

6

I fell into a routine, rising from my lair after the sun had set and the office workers had left the building, to hunt for blood. With several fresh pints coursing through my body, I would stroll the humid city, walking along its avenues, admiring the buildings and observing the people. I even did a little window-shopping. When I found something I admired, such as a beautiful jacket or a fine shirt, I would make my way quietly into the darkened store after hours and help myself to what I wanted. Sometimes I found cash in registers, which I would take. Before long, I had replaced the tight jeans and t-shirt and sandals with several jackets, a dozen pairs of slacks, some jeans, a number of dress and casual shirts, a pair of brogues, a set of tasseled loafers, and a couple of pairs of sunglasses (to hide the glow in my eyes). I'd carry the loot back to my hideout beneath the old office building, where I would store everything in an empty box next to my informal crypt.

For a while I took to skulking near the Hotel Rex, where officers and newsmen crowded the rooftop bar. I told myself I was just waiting for a victim to present himself to me. And each night for a week I would select and feast on whichever poor soul happened to stumble out of the hotel sloshed enough to make for easy prey. But in truth I was screwing up my courage to go upstairs and mingle. My loneliness was almost as great as my blood lust.

Early one evening, I pushed down my worries, strode briskly into the building, and made my way upstairs to the crowded watering hole at the top. I had barely walked into the bar when I realized I hadn't yet fed for the night. Already this wasn't going well. Gazing about at the knots of men standing and sitting, talking loudly, drinks in hand, smelling of booze and blood, I was overwhelmed by my hunger. Impulsively I followed a captain as he walked toward a tiny restroom. I pushed inside with him and closed the door.

Startled, he turned and growled, "Hey, buddy, I'm here first!" But I put a hand to his mouth, clamped my teeth onto his neck and practically inhaled his blood; he was dead within seconds.

Well, that was delicious. But I had ruined my entrance back into society. Now I had to find a way to dispose of the body without being noticed. It was a simple matter to carry the man under one arm, but there were no avenues of escape: every room and hallway was filled with humans. I decided to bluff it out. I rinsed off the dead captain's neck wound as best I could, slung one of his arms over my shoulders, and made my way patiently through the crowd, as if escorting a besotted reveler back to his room. His skin was pale white from the massive loss of blood, but I hoped others would figure he had merely become ill from too much drink. One Vietnamese waiter bumped into me as I neared the exit, asking, "You okay?" I smiled sardonically, rolled my eyes, pointed a thumb at the body, and said, "Yeah. He's just dead." The waiter nodded and turned away.

I fairly flew down the stairs one floor and walked silently along the hallway, stopping at each room until I found one my senses told me was empty. I broke the lock with one hand and slipped inside with my dead cargo, closed the door, and moved to the small window. It faced an alleyway. I opened it and leaned out, checked both ways, and, seeing no one, jumped – the body still in my grip – to land with a soft thump three floors below. Now I could travel at speed. In seconds, I was standing at the edge of the square in front of the Saigon Notre Dame Cathedral, its twin gothic towers casting fang-like shadows across the moonlit square. I placed the captain's body on a bench, arranging it so it would appear he had fallen asleep. I glanced up at the statue of the Virgin Mary that dominated the square. Her innocent eyes gazed heavenward while her bare foot crushed a snake. A chill ran through me. I thought, *Forgive me, Sainted Mother, for I am that snake.*

7

I decided the better part of valor would be to avoid the Rex Hotel. Instead, I returned to my earlier haunts on the crowded streets of the poorer districts, where drugs and sex were available at low market rates and expatriates filled the saloons. I made sure I was well fed before I entered these dens of humanity. I found that, sated, I could strike up conversations with anyone and not crave their body fluids.

In this way, over many weeks, I became a familiar sight at many of the clubs of the commercial districts. I would sit at the corner of a bar, order a ginger ale or water with ice, tip the bartender lavishly, then nurse tiny sips from my drink – I could absorb very small amounts without pain – over an hour or two, while chatting with whoever happened to sit next to me. I befriended Americans, Vietnamese, French, Chinese, Filipinos, even a couple of undercover Russians. My language skills had improved greatly, so that I now easily understood most of the tongues spoken in the city. I found I could eavesdrop on two or three other conversations while talking to someone at the bar. All this I enjoyed enormously. It soothed an ache I had suffered for months.

Most of the chatter was of war or bootlegging or politics or scandals. Now and then a visitor might, after a few drinks, blather on about the French philosophers or Theravada Buddhism or the possibilities of space travel. These conversations I enjoyed the most. They got me thinking about deep topics, the things I'd wanted to study in college, but without all the boring classwork.

Then one conversation changed everything.

I stood at the bar of a low-rent hotel, nursing my fake-beer ginger ale, when a voice behind me said, "How much of that can you swallow?"

I turned. He was short, stout, middle-aged, sweating slightly in a beautiful dark-blue suit. His hair was iron gray; his face, etched with time, was handsome. His accent had the flat tones of the American Midwest.

I said, "It's kind of warm for that jacket."

He smiled, nodded, and removed the coat. He tilted his head toward the stool next to me. "May I?"

"Of course," I replied. He settled in and signaled the waiter. "Scotch, rocks," he told him. Then, to me: "Would you like another soda?" I blinked. He shook his head. "No, I suppose you wouldn't."

Puzzled, I stared at him through my dark glasses. He smiled and offered his hand. "The name is Jager. Nice to meet you."

"John Smith," I replied.

He laughed. "Fair enough." He cleared his throat, leaned toward me, and murmured, "We are being watched."

I raised an eyebrow. This guy knew how to get my attention.

"Actually," he went on quietly, "it is *you* who are being watched. I am – how shall we say – merely the messenger."

A chill ran down my dead spine. I waited for him to continue.

The bartender set a glass of Scotch in front of Jager. Ice tinkled inside it. Jager paid immediately, as if he were in a hurry.

He said, "We have been watching you for a few weeks now, ever since we noticed all the dead people around town with fang marks in their necks."

I reached into my pocket and pulled out a wad of cash to pay my tab. Jager put a hand on my arm. "Please do not leave. We must have this little talk, sooner or later. Even if you leave the country, we will find you." He paused. "Your life depends on hearing me out."

I put my money away and leaned my arms on the counter. "Go ahead."

He picked up my glass of ginger ale. "You cannot really drink this, I know. It is a prop. As are your sunglasses – which, if I am not mistaken, are meant to hide the rather strange light in your eyes." He set my ginger ale down carefully between my arms and said quietly, "So we know what you are."

I felt the first real thrill of danger since the little

Vietcong vampire had transformed me. I picked up the glass and set it aside. "What do you want?" I asked.

"I want you to come with me."

"Come with you? Where?" This conversation had taken so many quick turns, I felt disoriented. And queasy. I looked at Jager, but he seemed out of focus. And then I was looking up at him. Behind him was the bar's ceiling. And then his face disappeared in an all-consuming blackness.

8

I was thinking about the old television sets from the early days of broadcasting. You'd switch them on, and after several seconds the screen would waken, displaying a wavering, unfocused image that slowly swam into coherence. I was reminded of that childhood experience because something similar had just happened to my own eyes, my vision opening up slowly, the edges wavering and undulating. I seemed to be lying on a couch. Dimly I could sense people moving nearby. My thoughts were dreamlike. I wasn't quite sure who I was. I couldn't remember what had happened before now.

I became aware of the cool, silky fabric of the couch. I began to hear things: a door closing, the clink of a fork against a food plate, a muffled dialog. Pain throbbed behind my forehead.

I sat up. The room spun. A man I didn't recognize walked into the room, stepped over to me, lifted my chin, examined my face, and walked back out. I sat alone for what seemed like a half-hour, though it could have been seconds.

Then another man walked through the door and took up a position on the adjoining wall, standing at parade rest. He was trim, of medium build, dark-haired, with a slightly swarthy complexion.

Jager walked in and sat in an easy chair across from me. He leaned forward. "How are you feeling?"

I opened my mouth but couldn't form words.

"Do not worry, it will come back to you," he said. "It is just as well, because I have a lot to say."

He picked up an oblong object and spoke into it. I recognized it as a walkie-talkie. Another man appeared with a large briefcase, which he set down and opened. From it he pulled a tripod and a film camera. He set these up behind Jager, aiming the lens at me. The camera began to whir. The operator adjusted it and left the room.

Jager turned to me. "The film is for our own purposes. We are not a news organization."

"Wha– wha' are you?" I mumbled.

"Ah, good. Your speech centers are intact. Sometimes the drug damages those parts of a brain in such a way that they do not repair themselves properly."

They'd drugged me in the bar! I hadn't even considered the possibility that chemicals could affect my body. I still had a lot to learn about my new self.

I licked my lips. "How?"

"Your drinking glass. The chemical is a mixture that includes the herb vervain. It has no ill effect on humans, so I spread some on my hand, touched your glass, and returned it to you in such a way that you were extremely likely to touch it yourself. I knew it would have a definite effect on a vampire."

The word jolted me. *So much for my secret life*, I thought. But I have always been practical: what was done was done. Time to accept my new predicament and deal with it.

I thought about the way they had poisoned me. "But I shook your hand."

Jager smiled. "The chemical was on my left hand. It's a damp material, and you would have noticed and, perhaps, been frightened off. We didn't want to have to track you after you had run several blocks and then lost consciousness. The glass, on the other hand, was already damp, which hid the chemical nicely."

I nodded; it made sense. I liked how this man's mind worked. "Okay," I said. "Now what? And who are you?"

"We are a private company specializing in intelligence gathering. The United States government is our principal client. You, by the way, are the third vampire we have monitored in Saigon. The second one cut quite a swath through the local citizenry about two years ago, doing much more damage than you have. You seem almost chaste by comparison. We approached him, but he refused our offer. It turns out vampires burn like dried-out Christmas trees, especially when doused with gasoline. He fairly exploded into flame. All that was left was a small amount of ash. No bones, nothing."

I stared at him. I remembered hearing, just before I shipped out to 'Nam, some stories about Buddhist monks here who had set themselves on fire as a protest against the war. One such immolation involved a Westerner, for some reason. I had given it no further thought. Until now.

I nodded. "What do you want from me?"

"We would like very much to have you work for us."

I had lost track of the number of times this man had surprised me. I chuckled, then laughed loudly.

"Why are you laughing?"

I shook my head. "This is all so ... so unbelievable. First, I'm minding my own business in the army. Then I'm changed into, well, what I am now. And then I find out I'm being followed. And they want to *hire* me." I laughed again, a bit hysterically.

Jager waited for me to calm down. "I can imagine," he said soothingly, "it has been a lot to take in. But you are an extraordinary being. And you are both extremely dangerous and extremely useful. To the right people."

I smiled sardonically. "I suppose you happen to be the right people."

"Well ... we will let you decide. We can offer you a rather lavish existence, along with our protection, in exchange for certain, how shall we say, *services* we might ask of you."

"And what would those be?"

"Oh, nothing you cannot perform easily. There would be little or no risk to you and a very large upside financially. Of course, you could use your skills right now to obtain most anything you want. But this work would in fact be a safer and more lucrative path for you."

"And if I refuse, there's always that big bonfire."

"Well, yes, there is that."

Were they bluffing? Could I escape and stay gone? Or would they find me, tie me to a stake, and light a match? Dizzy from the drug, I was in no condition to challenge them at this moment. Still, my situation made me feel trapped. Frustrated.

I stood awkwardly and began to move slowly around the

room. Jager stayed seated. I went to the camera, looked at it, and pointed it at the back of Jager's head. "Why can't I just kill you and leave? What's to stop me?"

Without turning, Jager said, "Theta."

I heard a thunk and felt a sting on the back of my right thigh. Immediately I had that wooziness I'd experienced back at the bar. I turned around. The man standing near the door had a silenced gun in his hands pointed at me. Idly I thought, _He must be Theta._ I collapsed and the room disappeared.

I awoke the same way as before, my vision wavering drunkenly to life, my body stretched out on the same couch. Slowly I turned my head; Jager's chair was empty. Theta still stood near the door. He saw me and rapped on the wall. The door opened; Jager walked in and sat in his chair.

He leaned forward, elbows on knees. "How are we feeling?"

"Like it was a great party."

He nodded. "You will come out of it, as before. We have removed the dart from your leg. The tip is a special alloy that can penetrate vampire skin."

I stared at the ceiling awhile, getting my bearings. I sat up, unsteady. I looked at Jager. "Okay, I get it," I said in a slurred voice. "You guys are well trained."

"My men come from some of the best commando organizations in the world, not just from America."

"Where's Theta from, Mossad?" I wondered.

"We will let the men remain anonymous unless a need arises for you to know them. It helps us do our work more efficiently."

Helps protect them from me, I thought. But then, so far they hadn't needed much help.

"Where are we, by the way?" I asked.

Jager sat back. "You're in a suite at the Hotel Majestic."

Still in Saigon, then. I knew the hotel, at least from the outside – a large French-Moorish pile that loomed, cantilevered, over an arched sidewalk arcade at the corner of a major intersection. I'd heard it was quite stylish and luxurious. Judging from the room in which I stood – elegant curtains, plush carpeting, comfortable seating – I'd heard right.

I rose stiffly, went to the window, moved the curtain, and peered out at the night. "So, what would you want me to do for you exactly?" I asked.

"Now and again, we might need your help in procuring objects that are otherwise difficult to obtain, objects that it would be in America's best interests to possess. Objects that her enemies might be unwilling to part with."

I walked back to the couch and sat. "So you want me to be your cat burglar."

He shrugged. "So to speak."

I looked at him for a long moment. On instinct, I took the plunge. "Sounds like fun. When do we start?"

9

"First, there are some ground rules." Jager and I were seated at a table in the hotel bar. A couple of his men lounged nearby. "For starters, you will no longer be permitted to hunt humans for their blood."

I looked behind me, then back at him. I pointed at myself. "Me? No hunting? It's how I live."

"You no longer need to. We can retain ample supplies of hospital blood for your sustenance. But we cannot have an agent who commits a random murder every night. That is not the deal we have with our client."

"Your client. You mean the U.S. government."

Jager shrugged. "This plan will not work if you ... *embarrass* them."

"Ah." I leaned back. "It sounds like you've hired vampires in the past."

"We may have had one or two on the payroll."

"So I suck on blood bags, steal logbooks and secret codes, and live the high life in this hotel."

"More or less." Jager sipped his drink. "And we will have to give you a new name as well."

I grinned. "John Smith doesn't cut it?"

Jager looked at me darkly. "We already know who you were before you were turned. You were a specialist in the Army, stationed in the central part of the country. But there is no need for the military to know we have located you."

"I ... appreciate that. I guess."

"Unfortunately I lost a bet, and I must assign you a name that's a bit awkward. But a promise is a promise. Your in-house name will be Christian."

I looked puzzled. "A Christian name? You mean a biblical name, like Matthew or Thomas?"

"No. *Christian.* Your new name is spelled C-H-R-I-S-T-I-A-N." Jager folded his arms defensively. For the first time, he seemed uncomfortable.

I laughed. "'*Christian*'? You're joking."

He smiled sheepishly. "The guy I lost the bet to, he has a wicked sense of humor. I would not have chosen that name for you, for obvious reasons."

I sighed. "Okay. Fine. Christian it is. Everyone will get a big laugh out of it."

Jager relaxed visibly. "I am relieved you see the humor."

I looked at him mischievously. "Maybe *you* need a name change, too. After all, 'Jager' is German for 'hunter.' A bit obvious, don't you think?"

"Let us assume 'Jager' is not my real name, either."

"Yeah, let's assume." I paused. "Although you did hunt me. And here I am. So it's apt."

Jager chuckled. "Yes. Now, there is one other thing."

"And that is...?"

"You may not ... you *cannot* ... contact your family back in the States. If they found out you were still alive, it would lead to, well, to your not being alive anymore."

I had kept it in the back of my head that, one day, I'd show up on their doorstep and there'd be a big reunion. Now the absurdity of that dream hit me like a ton of bricks.

I must have looked upset, for Jager leaned forward and said softly, "It is difficult to walk away from all that. But already they think you are dead. Let them be at peace with the idea."

I sighed. "I get it. There's no going back."

We sat in silence for a moment. Then Jager said, "Well, we should get down to business. You need to be trained."

10

And trained I was. For two weeks they kept me tucked away in their upstairs suite and taught me about locked rooms and safes and false IDs and surveillance and codes and communications and weapons. They even demonstrated some very impressive killing tools, in case my natural abilities somehow proved inadequate to a given job.

With my enhanced nervous system, I was a quick study. In no time, I had my new skills down pat. I memorized every manual and guidebook and map they showed me.

By day, they enclosed me in a darkened back room inside a very thick, heavy wooden box. Thankfully it wasn't shaped like a coffin; that would have embarrassed me. They also provided me with a couple of quarts of blood nightly, and that did seem to slake my thirst, so that I could tolerate the aroma of their own blood. I felt like a lion that's fed great slabs of meat so it doesn't devour the trainers.

After about a week, I could sense them relaxing around me, as if they had begun to conclude I was not a danger to them. I, too, relaxed somewhat. Frankly I had been just as concerned. This vampire business was still new to me. I was content to drink the bagged blood, though it was chilly and bland. It let me focus my endless curiosity on the subject matter at hand – how to be a professional cat burglar and spy.

Finally Jager announced that my initial training was complete. I would be free to come and go, with the stipulation that I check in with them nightly for any assignments. He said I'd receive a work order within a few days, but meanwhile I might want to walk about the city to refresh my sense of the place. "It's been a few weeks since you've been outdoors," he said. "We want you to re-acclimate yourself to the streets and people."

"Oh, I'm sure I'll be fine," I replied.

"I expect so. Still, it is good to get one's feet back under oneself, as it were."

He handed me a key. "Your rooms are just down the hall. The closets are fully stocked with clothing, and there is fresh blood in the refrigerator. Our people will restock and clean your rooms for you as needed. We have placed your sleeping box in the bedroom and have covered up the window, so you should be in no danger when you sleep."

I walked down the hall, unlocked the door to my new quarters, and stepped inside. It was a large suite, beautifully appointed, and provisioned as Jager had described. There were all sorts of clothes hanging in the walk-in closet, including casual and formal and everything in between. They even had placed a couple of pairs of sunglasses on the dressing table. How thoughtful. All this was good, because my old clothes were hidden away under the old colonial office building, and I'd had no chance to go there and salvage any of it.

I pulled a bag of blood from the fridge, uncorked it, and took a sip. It had the usual bland, unappetizing flavor of the chilled pints I'd been consuming lately. I wondered whether it might taste better if heated. I found a pot under the sink, placed it on the stove, poured in the blood, and lit the burner. In moments the dark-red liquid was lukewarm. I poured some into a glass and drank. Ah, that was much better! Still, though, it lacked a certain something. Live human blood has a flavor I can't describe that adds magic to the experience. This stuff, even warmed up, was a bit ... blah.

I changed into some nice slacks, a tailored short-sleeved shirt, and a pair of loafers – apparently they knew my sizes – and took the elevator to the main floor. I walked quietly across the cool, pale marble in front of the registration desk, and out the main doors.

The night was moist. Somehow the balmy air soothed me. I reveled in the liveliness and noise of the city. I let myself wander through the crowded streets, taking in the sights and smells and sounds of a major world metropolis that somehow managed to pretend it wasn't caught up in a dangerous war. With these people, life went on, no matter what. I liked that. I liked their spirit.

For a brief moment, I entertained the idea of running

away. With my newly honed skills and supernatural abilities, I would make a great second-story man. The world was open to me like a good book, and I wanted to read it all. But something held me back.

Was it fear of my handlers? I considered that and rejected it. After all, though they had cold-cocked me twice, I couldn't really believe they had the absolute power to stop me from escaping. Still, it was hard to be sure. Maybe Jager had made up the story about the other vampires. Or maybe not.

No, it wasn't fear that kept me tethered to them. Once again, it was my insatiable curiosity that had gotten the better of me. I realized I wanted very much to be a part of their team, and I didn't really care if the assignments were for the good of America or just extra-legal escapades. What I wanted was to have the experience they offered, the chance to play James Bond, the chance to do something really interesting. The chance to test myself in a new way. I was hooked, and I knew it.

11

The next evening, I knocked on their door. One of the agents opened it, turned, and said into the room, "It's Christian." He stepped aside and I walked in.

Jager was sitting at the dinner table, writing in a notebook, half-glasses for reading perched on his nose. Other team members sat near him, eating from take-out cartons. One of them pointed his chopsticks at the food and asked me, "Want some? It's shaky beef. Delicious." A couple of the men laughed. I rolled my eyes.

I pulled a chair out from the table, turned it around, and sat backwards on it, leaning my arms on the back, my chin on my arms.

Jager looked up from his writing. "How was your walk last night?"

I answered, "What, you don't already know?"

He smiled. "As it happens, we did shadow you. We were wondering whether you might decide to leave us."

I grinned. "I wondered the same thing."

He nodded. "Well, I am glad you are here as promised. We have no assignment this evening, so you are free again to wander about as you wish."

I hesitated. "There's something you said the first time we met. You mentioned three vampires in Saigon. One you burned, and one was me. Who was the third?"

"Ah, yes. Him. As a matter of fact, you probably know him."

Yet again he had surprised me. "Know him? How?" Then it hit me. "The Good Demon?"

Jager nodded. "That is the name they call him in the countryside. He is a short man, Vietnamese, very fast and cunning, and we could only obtain glimpses of him. We reckoned he was visiting the city to obtain supplies or information. Unfortunately, we lost track of him at the edge of town."

"And you didn't try to capture him? You know, put him to work like me?"

"Hardly. We suspect he is a very old, and therefore very powerful, vampire, and quite uncontrollable. Also, we have reason to think he is a dedicated Communist, if you can imagine such a thing from a creature like yourself."

Creature? The word stung me. Then I thought better of it. *Yes, I suppose I am a creature*, I thought. "I do know him. If he's who you say he is, he's the one who created me." I paused. "I always wondered why he did that. Why not just drink all my blood and kill me? Why turn me into this 'creature', as you say, and then let me go?"

Jager replied, "We think he despises Americans, perhaps from some odd loyalty to the human natives of his country. We believe he shaped you into a weapon he could aim at the enemy."

The nickel dropped. I was stunned. At last, the little man's actions began to make sense.

I stood and paced. The men went on eating, ignoring me.

Jager asked, "Did he say anything to you? Give you marching orders? Explain what he wanted from you?"

I stopped and faced him. "He warned me not to attack any Vietnamese. He said he'd find me and punish me if I disobeyed."

"Interesting." Jager pursed his lips. "Maybe, just maybe ... someday you can help us capture him."

I thought about that. The memory of him made me squirm. He had terrified me for twenty-four hours straight, and the idea of challenging him inspired nothing but fear. "I don't know," I murmured. "I'm not sure I could handle him."

"You would not face him alone. We would work as a team. Your powers would greatly enhance our chances. Perhaps someday we will have an opportunity. For now, though," he said, standing, "you are free to enjoy the city. Just check back here tomorrow night." He walked into the living room and shut the door.

I turned to go and noticed the agent who had let me in, still guarding the doorway. I was impressed at how quiet he had been, to the point where I had forgotten his presence.

Maybe they really were ex-Special Forces, or Mossad, or Russian Spetsnaz, or whatever. Maybe they had no need to bluff. Maybe I did have to be careful around all of them, no matter how skilled I became. My respect for them rose.

Then the moment got ruined. I was moving to the outer door when, behind me, someone said, "Don't eat any gooks." Another man sniggered. I whirled and blurred to the table in a fraction of a second. Through gritted teeth I hissed, "Let's not go there." Abruptly everyone stood, eyes wide, a couple of them drawing weapons. I reached across and snatched the dart guns. Then I laid them gently on the table.

The men stared at me. No one said anything. I glanced about to be sure there were no more tranquilizers trained on me, then turned and walked to the outer door. The guard opened it. I smiled blandly at him, glided past, and headed out into the night.

12

A few nights later, they had an assignment for me. I was ushered into the living room. Jager sat at his desk.

I said, "A job? At last?"

Jager swiveled in his chair. "I heard about the little disagreement you had the other evening with some of the team members."

I looked down. "Sorry about that, chief," I said. "It's just that ... well ... they got my goat."

"I understand. I have reprimanded the members involved. But since you are quoting Don Adams, I strongly suggest you *get smart* and avoid direct physical altercations with team members."

"I didn't touch anybody."

"You took their weapons. It amounts to the same thing." He paused. "I should point out that several of the men were still equipped to disable you, had the confrontation–" he paused, looking up "What is that new word? Ah, yes. *Escalated.*"

"Listen, if I were a normal human, I would have faced them down, even if I knew I couldn't win. It's, it's ... a guy can't walk away from that stuff."

Jager looked at me, tilting his head as if puzzled. "Interesting. You're a vampire, and yet... Of course you would feel compelled." He leaned back. "But I expect there will be no further trouble. From *either* side."

"Yessir."

Jager changed the subject. "As for your assignment, it's fairly straightforward. You should have no trouble with it." He explained there was a safe deep within the Chinese consulate building that contained some critical papers needed by the United States Central Intelligence Agency, America's chief spy group at the time. The CIA, in turn, had farmed out the task to Jager's team ... and Jager had chosen me as point man.

"We believe the safe has a standard dial lock. With your hearing, you should be able to open it in seconds. I can describe for you the specific files we want, but there is a chance of error, so we would like you to take everything – to be on the 'safe' side, as it were. As well, it is useful, now and then, to tweak the nose of the Chinese, if only to remind them who is boss."

At the time, the Chinese government centered on a malignant dictatorship that ruled one fifth of the world's population, but it had a very small and poorly equipped army, whereas America was by far the biggest military power on the planet.

"What if there's cash in there?" I asked.

"Take that, too. Bring everything here and we will sort it out. You can keep any money you find, but we would like to see it first, so we can learn more about how the Chinese do things."

Jager unrolled blueprints of the embassy, and for several minutes we studied the building's layout. By the time he rolled it back up, I had every square foot memorized.

The mental speed I'd attained after my transformation still dazzled me. I enjoyed it the way a teenage boy gets a kick out of driving his first car. I hadn't had time to explore the libraries in this city, but I was looking forward to it. I imagined all the interesting stuff I could learn, now that I was a speed-reader *and* a genius. Meanwhile, tonight's little jaunt would teach me new things ... and give me my first adventure as a burglar for hire.

The plan was to outfit me and send me off on my own – they weren't going to monitor me or establish two-way communications. Instead, my vampiric abilities were supposed to overcome any problems without their help. Frankly, I was eager to test myself.

Back in my suite, I found a set of black clothes laid out on the never-used bed. These I put on. Then I went to the bathroom mirror and smeared a blackening cream on my face and hands. Finally, I pulled a watch cap down over my pale locks and placed sunglasses over my glowing eyes. In darkness, I would be invisible to humans.

I opened the hall door, checked both ways, and quickly

retraced my steps to the team suite, where I knocked and they let me in. I glided over to the window. One of the men pulled it open for me. I glanced back at the room; the team members were all looking at me. I raised my thumb to them, turned, and dove out the window.

I landed in a crouch on a narrow service drive behind the hotel. Stepping to the shadows, I oriented myself and headed out for the consulate. I moved quickly, traversing entire blocks in seconds, unseen by pedestrians and bicyclists and taxi drivers. Within moments, the looming bulk of the Chinese office building rose up ahead. I angled around to a side door, expecting that, when I opened it, an alarm would be triggered. But with my speed, I figured to be in and out in little more than a minute. I yanked on the knob, breaking the lock, and a loud bell began to ring. I stepped inside and removed my sunglasses; despite the pitch darkness, my eyes could see quite well. In a fraction of a second I was at a door that, according to the blueprints, led down to the massive safe. I leapt down the stairs, turned, and saw the vault right where it was supposed to be.

I jumped to the safe. It was a Glenn-Reeder, a famous old box from the Twenties. How'd the Chinese end up with one of those? The dial was similar to a few I'd practiced on. I began spinning it. My vampire ears could hear the nearly silent action as the flies picked up the wheels, and my hands could sense the subtle change as each notch slid under the fence. I spun the dial back and forth until every notch was in place and the fence dropped home, freeing the bolt. I cranked the handle and pulled. The door opened.

Gas hissed from the safe.

Apparently there was a function I had failed to complete. Perhaps authorized users were supposed to flip a switch somewhere in the room or perform some similar act to disable the fumes. Fortunately the gas had no effect on me. I wondered what it would do to a human. It brought to mind the tranquilizer used by Jager's team, a chemical that *did* have an effect on beings such as myself.

The gas fizzled out. The vault cleared. Inside, I could see stacks of papers, boxes, a couple of small arms, bundles of cash – mostly dollars but also some Vietnamese dongs and

Chinese renminbi – and a tiny cage that held a cricket. The cricket was dead. *I bet that's bad luck*, I thought to myself.

From my waist I untied a black sash that became a large sack when spread open. I filled it quickly with the contents of the safe. I left the cricket. Then I stood, hitched the sack over my shoulder, a Halloween Santa in black, and turned to retrace my path through the building.

Standing silently at the base of the stairs, clad in black pajamas and slippers, stood an Asian man. Apparently he was waiting for me. I stepped toward the figure. His arms flew into action, and I felt sharp stabs of pain. I looked down; two of those little star-shaped weapons, used by martial artists, were embedded in my chest. I grabbed them and jerked them out, feeling more pangs as I did so, and hurled them at my assailant, who managed somehow to twist and duck, avoiding both weapons despite the speed and power of my throws.

I lunged toward the stairs, but somehow my feet flew out from under me and I crashed to the floor. He had tripped me! *Me!* Man, he was good. A foot planted itself on my lower back and pressed; I heard a loud crackle as vertebrae were crushed. For a fleeting moment I couldn't feel anything below the waist. I tried to stand but nothing happened.

I thought idly, *There go my legs again.*

Then my powers kicked in and my back repaired itself in seconds. I sensed the ruined parts moving into their proper places as the bones re-solidified, the heat of sudden healing warming the area to the point of pain. I wiggled a toe. Good! I flipped over, preparing to get up. But my assailant stood above me, a sword held over his head, its tip pointing down at me – *Where did that come from?* – and jabbed the blade through my ribs, piercing a lung and pinning me to the hard-wood floor.

Ouch.

I'd had enough. I was angry. I rose up, the floor-embedded sword sliding through me until its hilt was blocked by my chest, whereupon the tip popped free from beneath me and I stood fully erect. My assailant, astonished, stepped back. My hand darted out and grabbed him by the arm, pulling him sharply toward me. His shoulder separated with a pop. He screamed. I dipped my head and bit into his neck, sucking up a quart or more of his blood in seconds.

Ahh! I hadn't had anything that tasty in weeks.

I pulled back my head and howled. I bent to finish him, then thought better of it. The order had been clear: no drinking from humans. Already, on my very first assignment, I'd violated the contract. Somehow, I resisted the temptation to transgress further.

I looked down at the man. His body had gone limp from lack of blood, but his eyes were still alive, staring at me terror-struck as slowly I pulled the blade from my chest.

"Go to hell," I sneered. I raised the sword and sliced off his head.

13

"You broke a rule," said Jager.

I was sitting at the team dinner table, counting the cash I'd stolen from the Chinese safe. Nearby lay other parts of the swag: a pearl necklace, assorted rubies, and a pouch of uncut diamonds. I looked up at Jager.

"The blood-drinking? Sorry. I was in a fight. My instincts took over. But I did try to make it look like a garden-variety decapitation."

Someone at the table chuckled. Jager stared at the man, who looked down. Jager turned back to me. "All right, fair enough. Our intel described the victim as very pale, but there was a lot of blood on the floor, which seemed to satisfy the Chinese investigators. I think you are off the hook on this one. But next time, show a little discipline."

I raised my hand like a student. "I did stop in mid-feed. That's pretty hard to do."

Jager studied me over his reading glasses. "Hmm."

I pointed at the gemstones. "If nobody wants those, I'll take them."

Jager said, "Take the rubies and the necklace. You deserve them. You did pretty well tonight, all things considered. But we will keep the diamonds."

I pocketed the red jewels and the pearls, making a mental note that the division of loot from these operations seemed to be negotiable.

And then I made another note to myself. How quickly and easily I had changed from law-abiding citizen into murdering, thieving international criminal. And how little remorse or guilt I felt in doing so. I would never have believed in my earlier life that I could walk so easily down such a path. And yet here I was. I had taken to my outlaw existence like a fish to water.

I went back to my rooms and changed out of my skulking clothes. I applied cold cream to remove the blacking from my face. In the mirror, my eyes gazed back at me with their dead glow. If I'd been killed tonight, would that glow have disappeared?

I decided to take a walk. Outside, the streets were empty in the late hour. I strolled aimlessly. Somehow I found myself once more in the square in front of the city's Notre Dame basilica. Doing guard duty, as always, was the stone statue of Mary, her hands offering up the world to God, the globe impaled upon a cross. I sat on a bench and stared up at the statue. For a moment I wished I could chat with her, perhaps to make a confession of my sins. I wondered how the real Mary would have reacted to me. Would she have screamed in fright and run away? Would she have pointed her blessed finger at me in condemnation? Would her reactions have made any difference to me?

My eyes wandered over the square. I suppose I preferred the company of people to the quiet emptiness here. But I felt less and less a part of humanity. Their world was different from mine now. Their petty concerns and resentments meant nothing to a being whose abilities allowed him to indulge astounding whims. They were afraid of death; I was already dead. They were concerned about health problems; I had none. They worried about money; soon I would have more than I knew what to do with.

Yet I didn't feel superior to humans in any moral sense. After all, my new nature made me their enemy, their predator. I could hunt them – if not for blood, then for possessions. It seemed weird to think of myself as better than humans when already I had committed the crimes of a major felon and mass murderer.

And then I remembered the fight from earlier in the evening. Once I got into the swing of it, I was able to kill my opponent with little effort. Yet I was troubled by how easily he'd first disabled me. If I'd been a human, I'd have been a dead one in short order. For a moment he'd had me at a terrible disadvantage, which he failed to exploit only because he hadn't realized what kind of creature I was. Had he known, he might easily have chopped off *my* head.

It wasn't just Jager's team that posed a danger to me. Any human could defeat me if I let my guard down. As much as I didn't think of myself as better than humans simply for having certain strengths, I also couldn't assume I was invulnerable to them.

I would have to be more cautious in the future.

14

There were two more assignments for me that week. The first involved another theft of private papers from a very public government bigwig. The second job was a kidnapping.

The new theft required skills similar to the ones I used during the Chinese embassy raid. This time, though, the target was a private home – a South Vietnamese army general's home, to be exact – built decades earlier by colonials and commandeered by the southern army. This guy somehow had gotten himself on the U.S. radar, and our team was told to rummage through his personal stuff in search of anything that would confirm or deny suspicions that he was a turncoat.

I entered his living quarters just before midnight by way of the roof, jumping from a nearby building and landing quietly on the chimney top. I slithered down the crumbling, sooty tube and landed, again feeling like some macabre version of Santa Claus, in the very room I needed to reach. I was powdered in ash, but I had neatly avoided the alarm triggers placed carefully around the perimeter. Apparently the installers had neglected to consider attacks from chimney-climbing vampires.

The safe was a Remington hidden in the rear of a small Buddhist shrine. I had no trouble with the Yale lock, even in the darkness of the tiny alcove. Inside the vault, I found printed records, logbooks, a private diary, and some gold coins, all of which I snatched. As I jammed the goodies into my pouch, the room light flicked on. I disappeared behind a Chinese screen while the general himself – a stout, graying man – tramped in and sat at his desk. He flipped through some papers, snorting and picking his nose. Finally he sighed, put the papers back in a drawer, and walked out. I flitted over to the desk, opened the drawer, stole the documents, darted to the fireplace, and scurried up the chimney, all in about three seconds flat.

Sure enough, his private papers contained enough incriminating information to put him in front of a firing squad. "Again, nice work," Jager told me back at his suite. From the table where I had dropped the swag, he picked up the handful of glittering coins and tossed them to me. They flew across the room, spreading apart. No normal human would have been able to catch them all at once. But I was not a human. I had only to wave my outstretched hand to catch every coin in one move. I liked this vampire business.

The kidnapping operation came two nights later. A Vietnamese journalist had discovered some embarrassing facts about a high-ranking American official who had a weakness for the local call girls. The journalist wanted a large sum of cash to make the story go away.

We found his daughter drinking at a bar near the American embassy, though she was clearly underage. I strolled in and struck up a conversation with her. She was very pretty: she had the slender, taut body of a high school girl, with long, glossy jet-black hair that swung attractively as she laughed. I had little trouble adding enthusiasm to my effort to charm her. Still, I felt vaguely like a cradle robber. But this was Saigon. And I was a vampire. Pretty soon, she was well oiled and leaning lasciviously into me. I suggested we "walk over to my place." She obliged and put her hand in mine. I led her out the entrance and onto the noisy street.

We walked about a block. I turned left into an alley. Her hand pulled back, tense with doubt. I whirled, grabbed her arms, slung them tightly around my neck from behind, and began running through the streets at roughly the speed of a racing motorcycle toward the rendezvous point with Jager's men. It took less than a minute to get there, but the girl screamed the entire way. (My ears rang for a while afterward.) I dropped her at the feet of a couple of team members. They hustled her into a van and roared off.

I never did learn what happened to her. But the story about the American official did not see print.

15

The team quickly fell into a routine – if these little adventures could be called "routine" – of planning a raid, outfitting me as necessary, setting me loose to pilfer the objective, then either meeting at a designated spot or back at Jager's suite to evaluate the night's catch. Raids took place five or six nights a week. There was hardly any time to relax or explore the city. But I didn't mind. Playing James Bond was all the relaxation I needed.

I subsisted entirely on the refrigerated blood they provided. I became an accomplished cook with it, heating it to a perfect ninety-eight-point-six degrees and adding a dash of salt or nitric acid as needed. I found that my fascination with the aroma of live humans had faded. I hardly missed the thrill of the old hunt anymore – the anticipation as I singled out a hapless drunk or an American soldier who'd gotten lost in the rabbit warren of Saigon streets, the angry/loving excitement as my fangs plunged into the prey's neck, the almost orgasmically delicious flavor of the warm, red fluid as it coursed down into me.

Instead, the thrill of espionage became my new vice. First weeks, then months passed in this way, as I spent evenings running like a cat along walls, slipping in and out of buildings, creeping past sentries, defeating security systems. I got much better at avoiding alarm triggers until it became rare to hear an emergency bell. And always I would find and steal the items Jager required.

Well, almost always. One time I simply couldn't break into a vault at all. It was inside the Swiss consulate. I managed to sneak back out without incident, but I had to return to Jager's suite empty handed. Jager heard my story; instead of getting, angry he merely nodded. He said he wasn't all that surprised, given that the stubborn safe was in the foreign office of the country known for its timing mechanisms and other fancy small machinery. Based on my description of the safe, I spent the next three days poring over manuals and practicing until I could manage the likely locking mechanisms. On my return to the consulate, I did much better: the vault validated my rehearsals by clicking open smoothly to reveal a notebook that contained the secret Swiss bank-account numbers of several prominent Vietnamese business and army officials. I can only imagine how the Americans made use of *that* information.

I would have been happy to continue playing this nocturnal game indefinitely. One evening, though, Jager changed the rules.

"I need you to do something a bit different this time," he said as I lounged in an easy chair in his living room, burping from the blood I'd gulped down just before showing up for the nightly meeting.

"And what's that?" I asked.

"I need you to kill someone."

16

I stared at Jager. "Kill someone? I thought you said that wasn't allowed."

"We would rather you not freelance your murders, particularly if they leave evidence that proves we are employing a loose-cannon vampire." He paused. "But my client has no problem with you performing a sanctioned assassination, as long as it stays within protocol."

"Protocol?"

Jager pulled from a desk drawer a thick, spiral-bound book that had "Top Secret" emblazoned in red across the cover. He tossed it onto my lap. "Here is your recreational reading for tonight. It is the set of regulations the CIA has drawn up for covert ops – specifically, sanctioned killings. It is a bit dry, to be sure, but you will find it useful to know their rules. Especially if you are going to break them for me."

I flipped through the first few pages. It was dry, all right. Dry as a mummy. I looked up. "You said you wanted me to know these rules and then break them. Please explain."

"Well, I am not encouraging you to become an anarchist. I merely mean that, in so-called wet work, there often come moments when the assassin must improvise. Everyone involved understands that killings are messy affairs. But governments need to protect themselves. They therefore work up rules and regulations for operatives to obey. Then they can point to those rules, should an assassination become public and the legislature holds hearings into the spy agency's affairs."

"So it's a good idea to know what the protocol is supposed to be. Then I follow it whenever possible and make excuses for the rest."

"Exactly."

"Okay." I sat back and continued to read. With my vastly improved speed, and despite the extremely dense and boring text, I managed to get through the entire three hundred pages in about twenty minutes.

I dropped the book on the floor. "Done," I announced.

Jager looked up from his desk, surprised. Then he smiled. "Ah yes, I forgot. You are a vampire. You would have a terrific advantage, you know, doing scholarly work. In no time you could read absolutely everything in your field of study."

"Thanks, but no thanks. I'd rather go kill someone."

The words were out of my mouth before I had a chance to think. I winced.

Jager came over and sat on the couch. "This will not be a random thing. Target acquisition must be planned carefully. You will have to follow my instructions to the letter. I want no deviation from the opening script. Of course, you may have to improvise, as we discussed, after your target is acquired. But I wish to limit that as much as possible. Hence, the rule book, to start with.

"Oh, and, by the way... " He looked at me with a strange, impish grin. "There's a treat in it for you."

"I'm all ears."

"You have my permission, just this once, to kill as a vampire would, and to drink the target's blood. Just this once."

My jaw dropped. "I ... I don't understand. That's the big taboo around here. How come all of a sudden I'm free to do my thing?"

Jager raised a hand. "Oh, I am not giving you *carte blanche*. This is a one-time deal. It turns out that our client wishes a certain person to disappear. They have no requirement that a body be found. That part is optional. This leaves an opening for you. If you can dispose of the victim entirely, there will be no evidence that a vampire was involved. In that case, you deserve to have the treat."

"Aren't you afraid I might, I dunno, go wild? Get crazy, start killing everyone?"

"That is a possibility. Our understanding of vampires is incomplete. But I have watched you for several months now, and you seem too methodical a creature to give in to impulse. That is unusual for a vampire. However, it is a fact that you behave in that manner. It is clear you enjoy yourself immensely with whatever activity you engage in. But you always seem to show a certain discipline. You approach every task methodically. You have, how shall we put it, a very strong *work ethic*."

I'd never thought about myself that way. After all, hadn't I flunked out of college? But then I realized he was right. I had gotten straight A's in high school. I was the go-to guy in the platoon for recon. I was always organized, and the men often would come to me to help them find lost items, and Sarge had put me in charge of record keeping. And I'd dropped my early vampiric hunting habits like an old shirt when my situation had changed.

Jager continued, "Of course, I could be mistaken and you will make a fool of me. In that event, we would have to ... *terminate* your contract. With prejudice."

I put pressed hands to both cheeks and opened my eyes wide. "Omygosh!"

Jager snarled, "Believe me, I am serious! *Dead* serious."

"Okay, okay! I'm just kidding around."

"Please don't." Jager adjusted his tie. "On the other hand, should you perform this job well, there is a chance it might prove ... *useful* in the future."

"Useful?"

"I am not quite sure how. But it could come in handy if some of our future clients were aware that we had, on staff, someone with extraordinary abilities. If, for example, we had a problem collecting a payment, we might make them *aware* of the possible consequences."

I shrugged. "You're the boss."

"Very well, then. Let's discuss the target."

17

The target was another journalist. Apparently, suppression of information was high on the list of important matters pursued by the Americans in Vietnam. I assumed at the time that Jager's client list consisted of exactly one customer, and that every job was a part of the war effort, dirty though that effort might be. I later came to doubt my assumption: a few of the jobs seemed, on reflection, far afield of anything the Feds or the armed forces might conceivably have needed. Still, I never hesitated in carrying out the orders.

Except once. But I'll get to that.

The journalist, a very ordinary looking, middle-aged Vietnamese named Chinh, emerged from an office building one evening and joined the crowds flowing along the sidewalks. I followed, keeping well back to avoid detection. (As a light-haired Westerner walking down a street, I stood out like a beacon.) Our intel reported that the writer was in touch with a major news syndicate, and we suspected that tonight he would provide them with info the Americans didn't want splashed across the morning papers. I had to stop him before he got to the meeting.

How I stopped him wasn't important, as long as it wasn't in public and didn't look like the work of a vampire.

I bided my time, tailing him from more than a block away, focusing my ears on the sounds near him. Chinh strode purposefully, wending his way through the crowds, ignoring street hawkers, moving steadily, speaking to no one. He disappeared into a small grocery. I quickened my pace, entering the store moments later. I browsed aimlessly among the shelves while the target stood at the counter, dialing the store telephone. He murmured a few sentences into the mouthpiece, speaking Vietnamese. I caught a number: "nine-fifteen". I assumed that was the meet time, in less than ten minutes. Chinh hung up and walked out. I followed.

My job was to prevent the meeting – to put an end to all the target's meetings forever – and my window for this was the next nine minutes. I waited until he turned a corner, then I moved with a tiny burst of speed until I was right behind him. I knew this street, knew there was a short alley between buildings up ahead. That's where I wanted him.

I caught Chinh just as he passed the alley. I angled in front of him, blocking oncoming pedestrians' view of him, then turned and walked into the alley, my arm around his back. He looked up at me, startled. I grabbed his arms, swung him up onto my back, and begun to run.

I leapt onto a roof above the alley and jumped to the next roof, took two long strides to the other side of that building and leapt to the next roof, and so on, taking care to avoid power and phone lines, until I was standing near a tall building downtown. I caught both his wrists in one hand and used the other to climb the side of the building until we were at the top.

I set him down on the flat roof. He made no move to escape. Somehow he knew my purpose. He looked at me with eyes filled, not with fear, but with resignation. I rather admired him for it.

"Sorry," I said in my rough Vietnamese, "Just business."

He peered into my eyes, then nodded as if confirming something. He said in English, "You are a demon."

I thought, *Gee, except for the roof jumping and scaling this building, I thought I hid it pretty well.* Fatuously I asked, "Why do you say that?"

"Your eyes."

"My eyes make me a demon?"

Chinh shrugged. He said, "This is because of my work."

I didn't say anything.

He reached into his pocket and drew out a small notebook. He held it out to me. "This contains my home address. My family needs to know. About you."

I stared at him, then shook my head. "I can't do that."

Impulsively, he grabbed my arm. "They know about demons. One of–" He hesitated. "One of our relatives is a demon. The family does not speak of it to others. But it will

57

help them to know of you."

Interesting. Still, I pulled my arm away. "No promises."

Again he got that sad look on his face. I looked into the distance for a moment, then took the notebook from his outstretched hand and put it in my pocket.

I felt uncomfortable with the way this job had evolved. It was giving me the creeps. And I was a demon, as he had put it. *He* was supposed to feel creepy, not me.

Enough fooling around, I thought. I grabbed him by the shoulders. "This will only hurt a little bit." I must have sounded like a doctor about to give a shot to a patient. His eyes widened in alarm.

My fangs dug deeply into his narrow neck, nearly reaching to his spine, and I drained half his blood in one quick swallow. *My God, that was delicious!* I wanted to continue drinking and empty him, but I managed to restrain the urge. Instead, I took a deep breath, held his limp form, and waited. His eyes were rolled up in their sockets. After half a minute his heart fibrillated. Then it stopped beating.

I took Chinh's body to the edge of the roof. Down at street level, a fence topped with wrought-iron spear points jutted up from the ground. I held the body out over the roof edge so it would fall directly onto the top of the fence. I let go.

It worked better than I had hoped. Falling, the head dipped forward so that, when the body struck the fence, the head got nicely mangled among the iron spear points.

I jumped off the roof, floated down several stories, and landed a bit hard on the concrete walkway next to the fence. The body was well impaled, the head and neck pierced and ravaged, the rest of his blood seeping down the fence posts to puddle on the concrete. The police would rule it a suicide or a political killing. But now we had the notebook; no one would make the connection to us or our client. And no one would wonder, with all the devastation to the victim's face and neck, about some obscure punctures to his right carotid artery.

I felt a childish pride in my work. I also noticed a nagging tug on my conscience. I pulled out the notebook and flipped through it, reading the points Chinh had outlined for his meeting with the wire service man. The journalist had developed some juicy tidbits about high-ranking officials in the American embassy, wonderful stuff that made me chuckle with amusement, and a couple of shockers connected to the American administration that had me gasping in astonishment. Then I noticed the street address written into the front of the notebook. He had family who now waited in vain for his return.

I walked back to the hotel thinking, *This time, the good guy got killed and the bad guys got away with it.* I was grateful to be dead; otherwise, I might have been offended by it all.

18

The killings took place only once in a while. Mainly, I continued to perform thievery for Jager's team. Our chief American "client" remained shrouded – I didn't know exactly which agency paid our bills. And I never knew for sure that our work benefited America and not merely some high-ranking official's personal interest. War is a nasty business, and I had to assume that most of my assignments helped our side. But my interest was idle. I was, after all, a vampire – by nature, a hunter of humans, not a helper – so why should I care?

On the other hand, a promise is a promise. True, I hadn't actually *said* I'd contact Chinh's family. But I'd taken his notebook with their address scribbled onto the inside cover.

I gave the book to Jager but remembered the address. I had trouble facing up to the obligation, so I stalled for a few weeks. Then, one free evening, I walked to the Notre Dame basilica, slipped in through a side entrance – I got a small thrill as a vampire skulking in a holy place – and ghosted over to the apse behind the altar, where I hid until a team member walked in through the big front doors. Evidently he was assigned to shadow me. He walked down an aisle and stopped before the altar. He looked around, puzzled, then turned and walked out. I waited five minutes. Then I slipped out through a back door.

The dead man's family lived near the edge of the city, a few miles from where I stood. I decided to waste no more time, so I sped through the streets, a nearly invisible blur, and arrived at their door in about three minutes.

The ramshackle house was tiny by American standards. It shared a row of small huts perched on the edge of rice paddies that hazed into the distance. A ceramic wind chime hung from an eave. I reached up and brushed it with the back of my hand; it tinkled merrily. A moment later the door opened. A wizened woman, her hair battleship gray, stared up at me questioningly. Then her face froze in shock. She took a step back. "Demon!" she hissed.

This whole family seemed to have a thing for my kind. I almost felt flattered. And worried. What kind of alarm would she sound? Would she scream? Attack me with a knife?

She struggled to push the door closed. I raised a hand and stopped it. "Wait!" I spoke in halting Vietnamese. "I have message ... from Chinh."

She stopped and stared at me. "My son?"

Ah. Quickly I went on in her language. "He say he dead by hand of demon. Say demon in family also. Say you understand."

"You kill him?"

Well, who else? "Very sorry. War."

She looked away. "Now I know why he died. The government would not tell us." Her voice resonated with sadness. Then she looked up at me, her eyes narrowed. "You kill us, too?"

"No. Not war."

She kept staring at me, sadness mixed with puzzlement. There was no fear in her face. Apparently she *was* familiar with my kind and had somehow gotten used to us. "Why come here to tell us? You are a demon."

I sighed. "Make promise."

"To my son?"

"Yes."

She thought about this for a moment. Then she nodded. "You are like the Good Demon."

The mention of his name startled me. I recovered, but not quickly enough.

She gasped. "You know the Good Demon?" She pushed the door open wider. I was afraid she'd invite me in for tea.

"Yes. Know Good Demon." What else could I say? She was reading me like a book.

The old lady considered this. "You say you kill my son in war. But you are sorry."

I shrugged. "War is ... war."

"Strange, for a vampire." She made a quick mental calculation. "Then I forgive you."

My jaw dropped. I clamped it shut, not wanting my

fangs to interfere with her generosity. "Uh. Thank you."

There was nothing else to do. I turned to leave.

I felt a hand touch my arm. "Wait."

I turned; she was gone. I heard sounds of rummaging from within the tiny house. Then footsteps, and she was back at the door. She handed me a picture. It showed a young Vietnamese woman, very pretty, perhaps eighteen, staring into the lens, an enigmatic smile on her smooth face. I felt a twinge of arousal. Looking at her reminded me of the prettiest girls I had sought out in Saigon during military leave. But she didn't have the hard edge to her that most prostitutes displayed.

"My daughter. Her name is Ai Phuong. Very beautiful girl, so demons took her."

"Vampire kill her?"

"No. She is alive. She is a demon, too."

So this Ai Phuong was the vampire in the family, the one Chinh had mentioned. His sister! I looked again at the photograph; I couldn't detect the major telltales of vampirism – her skin was light olive, eyes a normal dark brown. "But she look human."

"She was turned soon after this picture." The old woman gazed down at her child's image, rapt, sad, for a moment oblivious of me.

I cleared my throat. She looked up. I said, "Sorry."

"But she is alive!" Suddenly she was angry. She grabbed my arm tightly, like her son had. Tears began streaming down her face. "Why did you not make him one, too?"

I stared. "Make Chinh vampire? That ... crazy."

"Not if he stays alive!" she wailed, and leaned her head against my arm, sobbing.

This was getting weird. Gently, I lifted her head away from me and took a half step back. "It was war," I repeated.

She sniffed and nodded. Then she brightened. "You must find Ai Phuong! Tell her to come home."

I had barely seen one vampire in my short career. How on earth would I find another? In this sense, Jager probably knew more about my kind than I did. I made a mental note to bother him about other vamps in the world.

I looked down at the old woman. "Vampires ...

dangerous. They kill."

"You do not! Not always," she said triumphantly.

She had me there. My current rules of engagement forbade it, though I could smell the fragrant temptation of the warm blood just beneath her skin. If I were a self-respecting monster, I would go out and kill and drink with abandon, starting with her. Instead, I had tethered myself to human handlers who had other plans for me. Either I was an especially wimpy vampire or a very disciplined one. I didn't know which.

The old lady continued. "And not her! Ai Phuong never hurt us. She visited here once, many years ago. We were unhappy that she was a vampire, but glad she was home. Then she disappeared. We have not heard from her since. Please," she begged, tightening her grip on my arm, "find her! Send her home!"

So weird. I would never in my human life have imagined a conversation like this. I was having trouble believing it now. A human family that wants its demon back, and a mother who buttonholes a vampire. I wanted to laugh. Or cry. "If see Ai Phuong, will give message."

The old lady relaxed visibly. She smiled and patted my arm. "You are a good demon! Good demon!"

Now I felt like a pet dog.

It was definitely time to go. I backed up a full step, nearly knocking over a small chair on the stoop. She let go of my arm. "Goodbye," I mumbled.

She nodded vigorously. "Goodbye! May the gods protect you!" She smiled and bowed and disappeared into her little house.

I turned and walked back up the street, surrounding myself with the sights and smells of the dark, strange city, wondering again what my place was in this roiling storm of warfare and treachery and deceit and fangs, where the love of family can lead to forgiveness for two monsters. I felt swept up like a leaf in the storm. Despite my new powers, despite knowing how to do my work and what my limits were, I had no real feel for determining my own fate, for knowing how to navigate through the maelstrom.

It was as if I were floating in free fall.

19

"So, what do you know about vampires?" I asked. I was sitting on the couch in Jager's suite, playing a hand of solitaire on the coffee table.

Jager looked up from his desk. "Not much," he answered. "What, in particular, do you wish to know?"

I sat back. "Well, for one thing, how many of us are there?" I had been living and working in Saigon for nearly a year now. I was beginning to wonder about the rest of the world, and where my kind existed on the planet.

"Our sources have estimated that the total number of vampires is fewer than four hundred, with a standard deviation of about ninety."

I did the arithmetic. "So probably between three-ten and four-ninety?"

"Correct. But those numbers are glorified guesses." As Jager spoke, he continued to write in a notebook. He had that rare ability to perform two entirely separate mental activities at the same time and do them well. I could do it, too, after a fashion. But I cheated: I was a vampire. We could do all kinds of things impossible for most humans.

I turned over a few cards. "How did you get those numbers?"

Jager kept writing. "Our sources took field reports of all known encounters, used some statistical heuristics, and extrapolated the results. But our current estimates are vastly different from the ones we were using just five years ago."

"Different? How?"

Now Jager set down his pen and swiveled his chair to face me. "About that time, some sort of plague – a virus, perhaps – swept through the vampire community. We believe almost seventy percent of the creatures died within two years. How the illness managed to infect them so quickly, given the relative scarcity of their numbers and the fact that they tend to keep to themselves, is still a mystery."

"Did you – how do they say it – isolate a germ?"

"No. Field operatives began to encounter vampire corpses, or what was left of them, in underground vaults and other darkened places. Usually when vampires die they dissolve right away. The years of decomposition of a normal body suddenly catch up with them all at once. But these bodies merely rotted, often drying into dessication, like mummies."

"So something was killing them, but you don't know what."

"Basically. Our best guess, as I have said, is some sort of disease process."

I frowned. "I thought vampires were dead. How do they get sick?"

"We assumed they did not until recent events told us otherwise. But we do know that vampires differ from each other genetically, and therefore phenotypically. They each have unique reactions to their environment."

"Pheno– What?"

"Their bodies, or phenotypes, display individual characteristics outwardly that hint at their internal genotypes." He smiled wryly. "Apparently you fell asleep during high school biology. My point is that vampires are not all the same. Many will burn instantly in sunlight, while others merely get a tan. Most are unthinkingly ravenous predators, but others, like you, are able to distance them-selves from their own desires. And the balance of them, apparently, are susceptible to an illness. But not all."

I stood, walked to the window, and glanced out. The alley looked just as dark and unfriendly as always. "Am I in danger from this disease?"

"Frankly, we do not know. You became a vampire after the epidemic had played itself out. We have no way, currently, of ascertaining whether you are immune or not."

I frowned. "That's no fun – something could kill me at any moment. I don't like it."

"Welcome to the human race," Jager said, smiling. "As it were."

20

The little crimes I committed on behalf of our American client continued pretty much non-stop. By now they often had me working seven nights a week. I didn't mind. I had nothing else to do, and I enjoyed the work. At least half the jobs involved safecracking, and I had become a fairly talented yegg. Often I could tell, just by listening to the whir and click of the dial, what brand of safe I was opening. I needed no stethoscope or other listening device, like human burglars. But with my increasing skills I felt a kind of kinship with them. I enjoyed the cool, solid feel of the door as it opened; reaching in to remove documents and cash and diamonds and gold bars felt almost anticlimactic. Oh, I kept any loot I found, after showing it to Jager. I never tried to embezzle it, partly because Jager nearly always gave me all of those proceeds anyway, and partly because I didn't care enough to try to circumvent him. The real prize was defeating the safe itself.

As an employee, I also received a goodly salary for my work. Jager had worked up a complete fake resume for me, and the deposits helped legitimize it. Meanwhile, the extracurricular "earnings" from the night jobs had long since outgrown the hotel safe. With help from Jager, who had people in Switzerland he trusted, I made some international phone calls and arranged for a Swiss account and safe deposit to hold the booty. I shipped the items, a few at a time, to the bank, insuring the packages and relying on the Swiss managers to be honest enough to place them unquestioningly into my private vault. I wired some of the cash, too, but kept back more than enough to handle my daily needs.

I had few desires that could be satisfied with money, but those tended to be expensive: fine watches, beautiful clothes, costly sunglasses. Mainly, though, the money and swag simply piled up in Switzerland. Before long, I had become fairly wealthy. I liked the power it represented and the freedom it promised. But for now my needs were few, and the wealth was merely a bonus.

The team and I got along. Whenever we had to work as a group, things invariably went smoothly. They were professionals – and so, apparently, was I. It felt good to be a part of something, however unusual, that required my talents and challenged me every day. It was a kind of game, and I kept winning. To my mind, this whole adventure beat all to hell lurking in alleys, waiting for suckers to suck. Yes, it was strange to be a vampire who didn't hunt. But it made me happy.

And then Jager dropped a bomb.

"We have another target for you to eliminate," he said one evening.

I shrugged. "Fine."

He shook his head. "This one will be difficult. It is a vampire."

I stared at him. "There's more than one of me in town?"

"Yes."

"The Good Demon?"

"No. Another. And this one has crossed us and gotten away with it."

"Gotten away with– There's been another vampire all this time and you said nothing? I'm so honored to be in the loop here."

"Don't be petulant. We found the creature only a few days ago, tried to make contact, and were rebuffed. And in the process, one of our outside contract agents was killed."

"Oh." I didn't know what else to say. I wasn't sure how to wrap my mind around this new information. And I hadn't known we worked with "outside contract agents" – whatever they were.

"We cannot afford to have such a being roaming freely, especially in our neighborhood. For one thing, it has caused us damage. For another, it remains at large, which makes us look bad."

I was confused. "Look bad? Nobody even believes vampires exist. Why would anyone blame you for something they think is a fiction?"

Jager smiled. "Our main client knows full well what is going on. If we cannot handle a rogue vampire, they will question our entire operation. Especially, they will wonder–" and he pointed theatrically at me "–whether it is safe to continue working with *you*."

I snorted. "Oh, so now *my* life is on the line if I don't kill this other vamp. That's sweet."

"We don't like it any more than you do. All of us are in danger because of this rogue. And we won't expect you to handle the situation alone."

21

The plan was to set a trap for the vampire, using me as bait.

About a mile from the hotel, in an area familiar to our target, lay a very small park, maybe fifty feet on a side, at the corner of a major intersection. By day it was filled with street vendors, but at night it sat largely vacant, its thick tropical plantings looming over a couple of old benches. I was supposed to sit there, a human corpse draped over my lap, the tableau spattered with blood from a bag normally used to feed me. The corpse would come from the local morgue. It was my idea to warm the blood, adding a touch of realism. We were hoping the other vampire would be drawn to the odor the way a shark – its senses alert to the slightest tinge of blood in the water – swims from miles away to inspect a wounded animal. Team members would take cover nearby, armed with telescopic rifles loaded with tranquilizer darts. They would fire on the vampire when it got close enough, and I would follow it until it lost consciousness and stopped moving.

I argued with Jager that the set-up was obviously fake and wouldn't fool the vampire. Jager replied that curiosity would win the day: "Vampires, like all hunters, are nosy. This little passion play will make our quarry want to know *why*."

I shrugged. "I guess you know vampires better than I do." Maybe he did.

We set up shop after midnight. I had fed from a few blood bags, so I felt sated, which would add to the realism. A small group of us piled into a delivery van. In the rear lay the shrouded corpse we would use. Jager unwrapped it. It was a young male Vietnamese, the body cold from the morgue. We hoped it would warm back up in the tropical heat. While we rode, I spattered blood from a heated bag onto my chin and the corpse.

About a block from the tiny park, the van's rear door opened and I slipped out, carrying the body. In seconds I was standing in the center of the park. The benches faced each other. I sat on one, arranging the dead Vietnamese over my lap, and waited.

One thing I can do for hours is sit still. Jager said vampires tend to be good at that; after all, why fidget when you're dead? I sat there till three in the morning, and then a flicker from a nearby flashlight told me to pack it in. I brought the body with me the short distance to the waiting van. The corpse was a loaner and we had to return it.

The next night we did the same thing with a fresh body. It got to about 2:30, and I would have stifled a yawn had I been alive, but then suddenly someone was sitting across from me. Even with my enhanced eyes, I couldn't quite make out the face beneath the conical *non la* farmer's hat.

"You broke your promise," he said quietly in Vietnamese. I knew the voice. The Good Demon. A thrill of fear ran through me. It hadn't occurred to me how this little scene would damn me in his eyes.

Quickly I said in my stilted Vietnamese, "I not kill! Body come from others. I wait with body for ... enemy."

I could see his features a bit more clearly now. His eyes were squinting, as if he were peering carefully at me. He looked at the body, then at me again. Suddenly he was standing behind me, bent over the bench, sniffing the blood I'd spread over everything, then sniffing the corpse.

He straightened. "You did not kill him."

"No."

"Then why–" He stopped. "You are hunting me!" he hissed.

"No!"

"No? Then..." He paused. "You are hunting *her*."

I was startled. "Her?" But the Good Demon was already gone.

That guy was quick. No wonder Jager couldn't catch him.

Then it struck me that the Demon hadn't been speaking in the abstract – the "her" he spoke of was already in the park. I don't know how I got that feeling, but I looked around. And there she was, standing just inside the tree shadows near the boulevard, looking at me.

Her hair was black and long and shiny; her skin was a silky, very pale olive; her face was mesmerizingly beautiful. I recognized her. The girl from the picture the old lady had shown me. The sister of the man I had killed. Ai Phuong.

22

Forgetting myself, I stood up. The corpse fell to the ground. Impulsively, I called out, "Ai Phuong!" Her eyes widened in shock. She turned and ran. The instant she fled, a rain of tiny darts plunked into the dirt where she had stood. I thought, *Nice shooting, guys, but a bit late.*

I raced after her. She was fast, and if I were human I would have lost her in two seconds. As it was, I had to use all my strength to keep up with her. She ran for miles, hurtling along twisting streets, jumping onto roofs and over fences, sometimes even clanking sideways along corrugated walls. (I didn't know vampires could do that.)

Eventually I realized she was headed for the wharves of the big shipping port on the Nha Be River. I followed her about a block over, trying to hide my presence, not sure how stealthy a vampire could be with another of his kind. She pressed on, running onto a huge pier and disappearing into a warehouse.

I approached the building quickly, afraid she would lose me inside it, wanting to catch a glimpse of her as she moved within the structure. I rushed through the big open doors and immediately was knocked the ground.

She had ambushed me. I was pinned beneath her. I twisted over and lay on my back. Looking up at her, I cried, "Ai Phuong!"

She growled angrily and pressed me to the floor. I tried to free my arms, but she was very strong. Suddenly, she grabbed my hair, twisted my head to one side, and bit deeply into my throat.

All the horror of my encounter with the jungle demon came flooding back. I writhed, terrified, but her jaws were clamped to my neck like a pit bull. I could feel blood pouring out through the wound and into her mouth. In seconds a weakness overcame me. I felt lethargic, dreamy.

I did not wish to be destroyed so easily. I wrenched my

head to one side and bit into her arm. Blood gushed into my mouth. This was even more delicious than the blood I'd received from the Good Demon. This was like nectar. This was heaven.

Strangely, she grew calmer, though her teeth stayed latched to my throat. I kept my mouth on her arm, and for minutes we lay there, sucking each other's blood. I couldn't get enough. I drank and drank, and as I did I could sense feelings and emotions, as if I were drawing them in with the blood. It reminded me of my time as a hunter of humans, except these feelings were more intense, as if this female vampire had emotions far grander than ordinary people could muster.

Some of the feelings were acrid: storms of rage, dark clouds of hate, cyclones of fear. Soaring over them all, though, was one dominant feeling – loneliness.

And then I felt a surge of love. Did it come from me or from her? Mingled with the emotion were vague images of Chinh, of their mother, of other people I guessed to be family members.

Abruptly she stopped, pulled her teeth from my neck, and sat up. Her glowing eyes blazed into mine. She tore off my shirt and pulled the blouse from her own body. She leaned down until her breasts touched my chest and her nose was inches from mine. "*Mister Christian*," she cooed. There was a French lilt to her words.

How did she know my name? Had she heard it in my blood?

She licked my lips, cleaning the stains from them, then pressed her lips hard against mine. Her tongue flashed into my mouth, flicking against my fangs until blood oozed from the scratches. I kissed back with equal abandon; blood flowed from both our mouths. We kissed, swallowed, groaned, and kissed some more.

Ai Phuong rolled over and I lay on top of her. She pulled off her pajama pants and removed my jeans in one fluid motion. I looked down: I was hard. She grabbed at me and, moaning, pulled me all the way into her. Somehow it worked – blood lubricated us. She wrapped her legs around me, thrusting and growling and panting, kissing my mouth, sometimes sucking hungrily at my neck. I pressed her to me, my arms wrapped around her, moving to her rhythm, smelling her hair, looking into her half-closed eyes. A roar of feelings coursed through me.

Over and over, she cried out in inhuman ecstasy. In turn, I felt waves of intense pleasure very different from what I'd known as a human. I wouldn't have traded this for all I'd felt before. This was beyond all that. This *was* heaven.

After awhile her body grew still. We lay intertwined, licking the blood from each other's faces, kissing quietly. I ran a hand along her body and down her arm. The wound from my mouth had healed over and disappeared. Instinctively, I touched my hand to my neck; it was smooth and undamaged.

Ai Phuong sat up abruptly, pushing me over. I fell to the cold floor. She reached for her clothes and began to put them on.

"What?" I asked, nonplussed. "Was I that bad?"

She leaned down and stared into my eyes. "You were wonderful, *Monsieur* Christian." She smiled. "But I must go."

"Why?" I felt like a jilted teen.

She giggled. "You are trying to have me killed."

I couldn't say anything.

She rose and sprinted toward the gap between the huge warehouse doors.

"Wait!" I shouted.

She turned and looked back at me.

I stood, naked. "Your mother asks you to come home."

Ai Phuong stared at me, unmoving, for what seemed like an entire minute. Then she turned and disappeared into the night.

23

I walked back to my hotel suite. I was in no hurry and I needed time to think. What would I tell Jager? And how could I meet up with Ai Phuong again? I wanted to see her very much. But did she want me, or was I merely a plaything?

What would I do if Jager sent me out again to capture or kill her?

Back at my suite, I showered off the blood and the smells. I put my torn, smeared clothes in a bag, changed into new duds, and took the bag downstairs to the incinerator. I waited till I was alone and tossed the bag into the inferno.

I went back upstairs and knocked at Jager's door. One of his men let me in. I walked into the living room. Jager sat writing at his desk as usual. I flopped down on the couch and sighed.

Jager glanced over at me but kept on writing. It was eerie how he could do that. He said, "I take it you lost her."

"Yep."

"Full report, please."

Again I sighed. "She was too fast for me. I chased her all over town, too. That thing could run."

"How did she get away?"

I shrugged. "Like I said, she was fast. I followed her down to the docks, and she ducked into a warehouse, and as I walked in she hit me from behind with, I think it was a pipe or a two-by-four. By the time I could get back up, she was gone. I searched all through the building, but she must have run straight for an exit on the other side."

Jager tapped his pen rhythmically on the blotter. Then he put it aside, stood, and came over to the easy chair.

He sat. "There's something you're not telling me."

"No. What?"

"I don't know. But you're holding back."

I squirmed. "Well ... you never bothered to mention it'd

be a *girl* vampire! And a cute one. I had no trouble chasing her. I was curious. But you could at least have told me a little bit about her. Then maybe, you know, I could have made a better go of it. Maybe could've caught her."

"My men report you called out a name just before she ran from the park. What was that name?"

I feigned surprise. "Huh? Oh, that. For a second I thought she was someone I knew from back when I was a soldier on leave. I met a lot of girls back then."

Jager leaned back. "I see. What name did you call out?"

"Uh, lemme think. I think she reminded me of ... what was her name? It was Hai Long or Ai Dung or something."

"Not *Ai Phuong*, by any chance?"

He must have tape-recorded the sounds at the park. Maybe he filmed it, too. How much trouble was I in? "Ai– what was it?"

"*Ai Phuong*. My men distinctly remember you saying it."

I smirked. "Really. Well, I don't think so. I don't remember meeting anyone by that name back in the day. But maybe it sounded like that."

I drummed my fingers on the arm of the couch as if bored.

Jager pursed his lips, looking at me. Then he nodded. "Okay. If we get another chance, we'll try to capture her again. We may need your assistance."

I spread my hands. "Fine with me. But next time, give me more intel, so I can do a better job."

Jager smiled. "Fair enough. Okay, that is all for this evening. You are free to do as you please with the remainder of it."

I looked at my watch. It was quarter to four. "Maybe I'll just pack it in for the night."

24

Nothing happened about Ai Phuong for a week. Then Jager announced he'd located her. "She frequents certain streets where call girls ply their trade," he said from his desk. "If you go there, you may encounter her."

I was standing in the doorway. "Then what?" I asked.

"Then you shoot her. With this." He stood and brought a small case over to me. I opened it. Inside, a lightweight automatic pistol lay embedded in styrofoam along with several of the small darts the team used to subdue beings such as me. Jager pointed at the darts. "You load them into the magazine just like bullets. The magazine is adapted to accept them. Be careful not to touch the tips! They contain standard doses. Try to hit her twice right away. That should stop her more quickly than a single shot. Also, it lasts longer."

"Why don't I just nail her with everything I've got? Maybe that'd kill her." I resisted the temptation to smile at my very private joke.

Jager shook his head. "We have never actually tried that. But we believe extra doses simply extend the time a vampire will remain catatonic." He looked puzzled. "All of them at once? That would probably knock her out for..." he actually counted on his fingers "...for about two days. But two darts will suffice. Then you cut off her head. She should disintegrate."

I raised my eyebrows. "Disintegrate? You mean, turn to dust?"

"Ash is more like it. Then you bring some of the ash back to us."

"Oh?"

"Yes. You know. To prove you succeeded. 'Documentation', as bureaucrats like to say."

"Oh." I smiled. "Okay." I feigned eagerness. "When do I start?"

"Our intel is almost complete. Probably tomorrow or the next night."

It took three nights. That gave me time to think through what I would do if I found Ai Phuong. I used the first night to visit my old haunt at the French Colonial building. I checked the basement: my box of clothes and my sleeping crypt were still there, untouched. Upstairs I went to the library, where I gleaned the information I needed from newspapers that hung on poles in the news racks. I found a telephone, made a couple of calls, and left the building.

When I reported in on the third evening, Jager gave me quick instructions about the streets where the lady vampire might be found, handed me the little case with the trank pistol, and sent me into the night.

I glided through the city, my face blackened, my hair under a cap, dressed in my best black clothes and sunglasses. To nearly all the people I flitted past, I was little more than a passing breeze. I arrived in the district Jager suggested, jumped lightly onto a roof, and began leaping from building to building, my eyes searching the streets below.

I wondered whether Ai Phuong would see me before I saw her. But within an hour I spotted her first. She was stalking an unsuspecting sex worker down a dark alley. I watched as she waylaid the poor prostitute, dug her fangs into her neck, and sucked the life from her. The hooker's body seemed to shrink visibly as the vampire absorbed its blood, the skin turning from light olive to ghastly white even in the darkness of the alley. Ai Phuong dropped the body carelessly and ghosted away. I could see why Jager wanted Ai Phuong dead: her lack of caution would bring attention to her crimes and, with it, unwanted peril to Jager's private vampire. That would be me.

I darted over rooftops, following her. Ai Phuong roamed randomly, crisscrossing streets she had just passed over, arcing a mile away, then coming back to the same alley where she had murdered the prostitute. As I ran along above her, I thought, *She's the Jack-the-Ripper of Saigon.* Then I realized that I, too, had played a similar role, not so long ago.

I was closing in on her, planning to make a speed dash, leap off a roof, and land on top of her, when she stopped suddenly, turned, leapt onto the roof I was crossing, and faced me.

I skidded to a halt. "Ai Phuong!" I said, almost happily.

She smiled. "Mister Christian," she cooed.

I took a step toward her.

She backed up. "Are you here to kill me?" she whispered in her French-tipped English.

I sighed. "Yes and no."

"Yes and no? Please explain."

"They want you dead. But I don't. I ... I want to know you better. But Saigon is too dangerous for you. You have to leave." As I spoke I edged toward her.

Ai Phuong snorted. "Leave? I live here. I like it here. Your people are no danger to me."

I shook my head angrily. *"But they are!* Twice they have disabled me and could have killed me."

She smiled condescendingly. "You are young and weak. And you are their patsy."

Her words stung me. But she had a point. I said, "They have very clever ways of tracking and capturing vampires. They will find you eventually. You have caused them harm, and they won't stop until you're dead."

She grinned. "All the more fun, then." And she was gone.

25

I followed her at full tilt. Again she led me on a merry chase through Saigon. Again her run took her toward the docks. Again I saw her dash into the same warehouse.

I approached the giant doors, still ajar. "Ai Phuong? Ai Phuong? Please. Come out and talk to me. I don't want to hurt you at all. I want to protect you."

I entered the building. It was pitch black inside, but my enhanced eyes picked up enough glimmers to create a full composite of the interior. As before, it was huge and empty. I took a few tentative steps deeper into the gloom. "Ai Phuong?" I called.

A weight crashed down onto me. I sprawled on the floor. It was Ai Phuong, laughing, pushing me to the concrete, tearing off my shirt, snarling as she plunged her fangs into my neck. Again, a weightless sensation of languor overcame me. Again, the desire to live struggled to the surface. Again, my mouth found her arm and I broke through it and pulled hard at her blood, taking in pint after pint while she drank from me.

Beyond the blood, I could again sense a powerful current flowing between us – clearly the blood transferred feelings, even thoughts, as it flowed into our mouths and out our wounds into the other's mouth. The sensation was sexy beyond belief. And it had some deeper dimension to it, almost a spiritual thing, as if our souls were united, blending together as we drank each other's dark fluids.

Somehow, as before, Ai Phuong managed to strip the clothes off us with barely more than a gesture. As before, she rolled and placed me on top of her. As before, I plunged into her and she cried out, pulsing and thrusting and contracting around me and climaxing over and over, while I felt waves of ecstasy course through me.

Again we lay spent, idly licking up random streaks of blood from each other's skin.

I lifted myself onto one arm and looked down at her. Her black hair splayed out on the concrete in elegant disarray. She was beautiful, absolutely gorgeous. I wanted to keep her here with me, postpone what I had to do. But with what? Idle chit-chat? Ask about her family? Right, let's delve into how I killed her brother.

I leaned down and kissed her. "Ai Phuong," I whispered, "I do believe I have a crush on you."

She laughed. "Good. I like it when a man needs me. It makes me feel ... powerful."

She sure had a way of dashing my daydreams. It made her all the more desirable.

Ai Phuong wriggled out from under me. She pulled on the pajama bottoms and t-shirt she had worn this evening. I rolled to a sitting position and reached for my clothes, making as if to put them on. Instead I pulled the pistol from a pocket and fired it point-blank at her. Twice.

Shocked, she jumped up. "You bastard! *Merde de l'eau! Spece de conte!*" Her angry face clouded over. She wavered, dazed.

I dropped the gun and grabbed her shoulders. "I'm not trying to hurt you! But you must leave Saigon!" She twisted, trying to break free. But already she was weakening, her knees beginning to wobble. "Listen!" I said sharply. "I'm sending you out of the country. You'll be fine in America. I'll tell my people I killed you. I will *make* them believe me. You will be safe. But you cannot come back!"

Her eyes crossed, then focused. She looked up at me. A tear of blood trickled down one cheek. She put a hand on my face. Drunkenly she mumbled, "*Je t'adore,*" kissed me languidly on the mouth, and slumped in my arms, out like a light.

I placed her gently on the floor, picked up the gun, and emptied it into her, firing all the darts I had brought. I hoped such a big dose would keep her out long enough for my plan to work. I pulled the darts from her and dropped them onto the concrete. Then I picked her up and draped her over my shoulder. She was surprisingly light for so strong a being. But then, I had never bothered to weigh myself since becoming a bloodsucker; I had no idea how heavy a vampire was supposed to be. I walked to the warehouse doors and peered out. The docks were empty. Quickly I ran naked across the open space and headed up to the street. From there I traveled at a vampire's dash to a dock about half a mile away. In moments I found the ship I wanted, an American freighter scheduled to embark at dawn.

Holding Ai Phuong carefully, I leapt upward and landed on the deck of the freighter. I found a gangway and quietly dropped down the stairs and into the belly of the ship. Twice I almost bumped into crewmen, but each time I used my speed to backtrack, hide behind a bulkhead, and wait for them to pass. Eventually I worked my way down several flights to a level crammed with crates. I chose one at random, pried it open with one hand, checked inside – it was an empty, apparently on its way back to the U.S. for a reload – and placed the unconscious vampire inside it. I set the crate's lid back in place, pressing the nails into the wood with my thumb. I bent down to the lid and whispered, "Good luck, Ai Phuong. I hope we can meet again someday."

I glided back upstairs, jumped off the deck, landed on the pier, and headed back toward the warehouse where Ai Phuong and I had made love. Along the way, I scanned the buildings for any sign of fresh water. Outside a guardhouse at the land end of a pier, I found a barrel with a ladle. I poured water onto my lower parts, rinsing them off. I hurried to the warehouse. The gun and darts lay near my clothes where I had dropped them. Good. I set them aside, dressed, then pulled a switchblade, a canister of lighter fluid, and a matchbook from my pockets.

Abandoning Ai Phuong to a ship that would take her away from me – that was hard. But what I had to do next would be difficult in the extreme.

I bent down over the spent darts and, flicking open the knife, sliced into my left pinkie finger. Damn, that hurt! The switchblade was a mistake – they're good for sticking people, but the edges are pretty dull. I should have brought something sharper. Still, I had to go through with this, so I sawed away until the finger separated. Wincing, I sucked at the stump and hoped the finger would grow back. I opened the canister of lighter fluid, doused the severed digit, lit a match, and dropped it onto the finger.

It worked better than I had hoped. The fluid caught and burned briefly, then the finger flared up brightly with a loud hiss and was gone. Smoke rose from a small pile of ash. Idly I thought, *Those stories are true.* The darts were nicely coated with ash. I pulled a small paper bag from a pocket and carefully scooped up as much of the gray powder as I could. I collected the empty darts and, along with the fluid, matches, and knife, placed them in my pockets. Then I bent down and blew on the remaining ash. It scattered into the darkness of the warehouse. No point leaving evidence for some cop to wonder about.

As I walked from the warehouse, I discarded the fluid, matches, and knife, one at a time. I could feel my hand throbbing. I glanced down. Through the bloody stump where the pinkie had been, a knob of new flesh protruded. I could see it emerging millimeter by millimeter as I walked. I had guessed correctly: lost body parts *do* grow back on a vampire.

Thank God for small blessings.

26

I dropped the bag of ashes onto Jager's desk. He stopped writing and poked at it with a pen. "What's this?"

"Part of a vampire."

"Oh." He opened the bag and peered in. He sniffed at it. "How did things go?"

"She's dead. I'm not." Carefully, I placed the empty trank darts in a row next to the bag.

He looked up at me. My face was still covered in blood, my shirt still torn. He said, "It appears the rules got bent again."

"Oh come off it! I got her for you. It was a fight between vampires."

He put up a hand. "Easy, now. You are correct. You solved our problem. Well done."

"Listen, I don't mind doing your dirty work for you. It's just ... you should..."

"We should give you more intel in the future. Will do." He noticed my wounded hand. "What happened there?"

I lifted the hand, stared at it. The new pinkie was half grown-in already. "Nothing. I lost a finger during the fight. It's growing back."

"Really?" Jager rose and came over to stand next to me. "May I?"

I held out my hand. Jager took it, turning it this way and that, gazing at the wounded area. He called out, "Delta!" The door to the dining room opened and one of the team members – a tall, blond, Teutonic-looking guy – stepped in. "Bring the camera." Blond Boy walked out and returned moments later with a Leica and a flash attachment, which he handed to Jager. Jager examined the camera, made a couple of adjustments, then aimed the lens at my hand and, holding the flash slightly to one side, took several snaps.

"Have these developed," he said to Delta, who took the equipment and left. Jager went to his desk and made a few quick entries in one of his many notebooks.

"Keeping the ledger on your lab rat, eh?" I said.

Jager chuckled. "If you were merely a rat, things would be a great deal simpler." He put the notebook away and faced me. "Again, well done. You can go clean up. Be back here as usual tomorrow night. I will have a big announcement."

"What, I'm fired?"

He smiled. "You wish."

"Okay, then, we're all getting medals."

Jager stared at me over his reading glasses, his eyes withering. "Patience, Christian. All will be revealed tomorrow. We will be moving."

"Moving? What's wrong with this hotel? I was just getting used to it."

I wanted more, but he waved me away and disappeared into his bedroom.

Ah well. Jager loved surprises. I'd just have to wait. I walked out of the suite and back to my rooms, where I enjoyed a long, warm bath and a pitcher of heated blood. The evening's work had made me hungry.

As I lay in the suds, sipping the bloody brew, I tried to organize my thoughts. At least my story seemed to convince Jager. He had even praised me, which rarely happened. Maybe I was out of the woods.

I thought of her. In a couple of hours she would be at sea. I hoped, for her sake, she liked America. She could speak English, she was gorgeous, and of course she was a vampire. How hard could a new country be?

How hard, indeed. I was about to find out.

27

A team member answered my knock. I entered the suite.
The men were assembled around the dining room table,
some sitting, others standing. Jager looked up. "Ah, he has
arrived. Good."

I walked over and leaned on a wall next to Delta. He
ignored me. Jager made his way around the room, handing
out passports. When he got to me, he handed me a driver's
license. I looked at Jager quizzically, but he shook his head
and continued around the room. I looked down at the license.
It had a perfectly ordinary photo of me staring blankly into
the camera just like on a real card – how'd they get *that*
shot? – but my name was new. Adam Charles or something.
A mild joke about a horror cartoonist, as I recall.

"Your passports have been processed and stamped. Your
flight will leave tomorrow evening. Pack your gear and
destroy anything you must leave behind. I will have a team
go through all the rooms to give them a thorough cleaning,
but please save them some effort."

I had never bothered to wonder where the team members
slept. They had always seemed a little unreal to me, as if
they were wind-up dolls stored in a closet. Apparently they'd
been living in the hotel the whole time. By now I should
have noticed. What else had I ignored? Did they have
girlfriends? Did they sleep with each other? I imagined them
scattering to their respective rooms to burn incriminating
pieces of paper, flush chemicals down toilets, and cram
suitcases with clothes and guns and cameras. Was it part of
their training, never to be seen living normal lives? Or were
they merely hiding themselves from me?

Jager interrupted my thoughts. "You'll be landing at
Travis Air Force Base near San Francisco."

"San Franci– *America?!*" I blurted out. Everyone turned
and looked at me.

I had assumed we were moving across town, not across

the Pacific. Clearly, the rest of them knew more than I did.

My mind reeled. Part of me thought it was exciting to return to the United States. But another part of me was appalled. *Ai Phuong! I've sent you straight into danger! I should have left you in Saigon.*

I stared at Jager. "Nice of you to tell me."

He ignored me. "From there you will transfer by taxi, a few at a time, to commercial flights from Sacramento or Oakland to Burbank. Use the name on your passport to confirm the reservations. When you arrive in Burbank, take taxis to our new headquarters in Santa Monica. The Los Angeles area is fairly spread out, and the taxi rides will be costly both there and in Northern California." Jager handed out small stacks of cash to team members. "This cash will defray your incidental expenses."

There was more to the briefing – details about which hotel the men would bunk at, warnings about local statutes and drinking laws. I only half-listened. After twenty minutes, Jager dismissed the team but told me to stay. Most of the men filed out; two remained to stand guard. Probably watching *me*.

Jager peered at me over his reading glasses. "First, any questions?"

Well, *duh*. "How come I'm not in the loop? What else haven't you told me? You know, little details that could get me *killed*."

Jager straightened some papers and put them in a briefcase. "There is no reason to be annoyed. Your situation is different from the others. For one thing, you need much less time to prepare." He snapped shut the briefcase. "Also, we will do your packing for you. A team is in your room as we speak, preparing your belongings for shipment."

Jager walked into the living room. I followed. He set the case on his desk. I threw myself down on the sofa and pouted. Jager removed his reading glasses, placed them in his shirt pocket, and sat on the easy chair across from me.

He leaned forward. "You are a special case. We must handle you differently. I think you understand why. That does not mean I lack respect for you or your work. I have been very pleased with your efforts on our behalf. I expect to continue our relationship in California."

My anger was ebbing. "I suppose," I said slowly, "I would treat me the same way."

"I appreciate your understanding."

I looked up, a mischievous grin on my face. "I could just light out for, oh, Cambodia. Bet you wouldn't try to stop me."

He smiled. "Frankly, you are correct. It would be difficult for us to launch a mission to locate you while we were in transit out of the country." He sighed. "Personally, I would be sad if you did. I have enjoyed working with you."

I looked away, feeling awkward.

Jager continued. "But I am betting you will not. I think you enjoy this work, with all its perks, too much to walk away from it. Especially when we are about to embark on a new mission in a very desirable location."

He was right. Worse, I'd enjoyed working with him, too. He had been almost like a father to me. It embarrassed me to realize it, but here I was, the big scary vampire, and I would have missed my team, my little family. How quaint. Now I *knew* I was a pansy of a monster.

As my pique subsided, my guilt surfaced. Jager was going out of his way to be nice to me, and only the night before I had betrayed him, letting his target escape rather than destroy her as I'd promised. What would happen if she were to appear in our new neighborhood? Would I have to kill her, this time for real? Or would they simply kill me and deal with her later? I hoped there were enough vampires in the States to obscure any misdeeds she might commit. With so many such monsters in one region, maybe Jager's team would no longer be under the gun to find and dispense with them all.

Maybe. All I could do was wait and see. But I didn't like the loose end.

I was worried about one other thing. "You expect me to fly in an airplane? What about daylight? How would I survive?"

"You will not be flying. You have noticed we did not provide you with a passport. Instead, we have arranged for your passage aboard a freighter to Los Angeles. We will place a team member with you, should you need anything."

"A ship? But that'll take a couple of weeks! How will I eat? Do they have a nice refrigerator filled with blood just for me? Come on!"

Jager shook his head. "We will load you aboard in a travel trunk that we have constructed to your size. You will need to remain in the trunk, below decks, for the entire trip. Our studies indicate that vampires, in such conditions, tend to hibernate. We will awaken you at the other end, feed you immediately, and drive you to our new headquarters. Actually, your trip should be less uncomfortable than that of the other team members, as you should be peacefully asleep most of the way."

"And when I arrive in port? The customs guy drives a stake through my heart?"

My guilt was surfacing again. I needed to stay cool.

"Our team member will awaken you at the appropriate time, and you will disembark at night when it is safe. You should have no trouble evading the customs gate. As for your trunk, we have put in all the comforts. A mattress, a small ice chest with a couple of blood bags to get you started. Please drink them immediately, as the ice will melt and the blood will spoil. And we have placed a jar of earth inside to help you sleep. Apparently, vampires can become disoriented when away from land."

I thought about it. How hard could it be? And how else would I get to America?

"Okay," I said. "So when do I jump in the trunk?"

"Tonight."

"Tonight?"

"In an hour."

28

A short time later, I stepped into the main lobby of the Hotel Majestic. I was dressed in jeans and a t-shirt. Over my arm was a heavy jacket, intended for the cold of my upcoming sea voyage below decks. The outfit was completely wrong for Saigon and inappropriate for the lobby. But I wanted one last glimpse of the main floor of the place I had come to think of as home. My eyes fell on the long registration desk, and I realized I had never used it – my accommodations here had always been taken care of by others. I wondered what my new living arrangements would be like in California.

The doorman let me out the front entrance with a flourish. The intersection before me was crowded as always with the evening's bicyclists, scooters, small cars, and overloaded carts. I took a deep breath of heady, heavy Saigon air. Despite the crowding and noise and odors and humidity, I would miss this town.

I turned and walked under the gaily lit arcade to the end of the building, then turned again into a service alley. About a hundred feet back, a small van stood waiting. I walked up to it and rapped on the rear door. It opened; I jumped inside.

The van rumbled to life and rolled into motion. I steadied myself and squatted down between a team member – Foxtrot, they called him – and a large trunk intended for my use during the ocean crossing. Stenciled on its side were "US ARMY" and "THIS SIDE UP". I'd have wished for "FRAGILE", but that probably would have aroused more curiosity than Jager liked. Foxtrot unhooked the hinges and raised the lid. I peered inside: at the bottom lay a simple mattress outfitted with a sheet and blanket. How thoughtful! At one end was a small picnic cooler box. I opened it and saw bags of blood nestled atop a mound of ice. Next to the box stood a large glass jar filled with what looked like soil. Ah yes, so I wouldn't become "disoriented," as Jager had put it.

Foxtrot said, "You should get inside."

I nodded, tossed in my jacket, and rolled quickly and smoothly into the trunk. Hey, comfy!

Foxtrot said, "That was fast."

I looked up at him. "Yeah, well, you know. It's a gift." I felt along the sides of my little chamber. "Any air holes?" I asked.

"You shouldn't need any," Foxtrot answered. "You don't need to breathe, do you?"

I smiled. "No, I guess not."

"Better security if there's no way to see inside."

"Good point."

Foxtrot said, "Bon voyage," and closed the lid. I was plunged into darkness. I heard clicks as he closed and locked the hinges. I felt a moment of panic. Should I test the crate, kicking out the end piece to be sure I could escape in an emergency? I decided to trust the team's work – if I broke the trunk now, there might not be time to repair it. Also, they might think I was a jerk.

The van bounced and shook its way along the unevenly maintained streets. After about fifteen minutes the tires began making a rhythmic patter, and I realized we were driving across the wooden beams of a pier. The van slowed, then stopped. The vehicle lurched up and down as people got out. The rear doors squeaked open. Suddenly my trunk tilted, rose up, and began swaying rhythmically to the sound of footsteps. Like a funeral procession, they were shouldering the dead guy to a new resting place.

The trunk tilted again and I heard the hollow sound of footsteps on what I guessed to be a gangplank. The trunk leveled out and moved forward steadily. Then my impromptu crypt dropped with an unceremonious thunk. After a moment I heard a powerful electric motor buzz to life, and the trunk began to move slowly downward. I figured I was on a freight elevator platform. In a few moments the motion stopped. This time, the trunk was pushed, sliding along the floor for maybe twenty seconds until the head end slammed hard against something and stopped moving. *Hey, guys! Watch it!* The foot end swiveled around until it, too, banged into place. I heard footsteps walking away and voices I didn't recognize discussing the next shipping container. Already I was under the rather nonchalant care of the ship's crew.

In truth, their cavalier treatment of my little crate was good news. They had no idea a lethal creature lay within.

So far, so good. Now the big problem would be boredom. I entertained the notion of breaking out once we were under way and exploring the ship. I figured I could put pressure on my crate's edges and force them apart. But it would be difficult, once I'd returned to my sleeping quarters, to replace the screws from the inside.

While I pondered this problem, I grew inexplicably sleepy. It was still nighttime, according to my watch. But ... *yawn* ... there's nothing like turning in early...

PART 2

IN STATE

29

I dreamed I was on a sailboat that pitched and yawed its way across an endless sea. The sun poured blinding light and pounding heat down on me. I was alone on the deck of the little sloop, its mainsail and jib set close-hauled on a starboard tack. The sea air was fresh and balmy. I heard voices of men below, a couple of dozen. How could they all fit into such a small cabin? They spoke about weather and headings and rough seas and cargo safety and families and petty squabbles and sex and food. I gazed at the horizon all about me: in no direction could I see any sign of land. No gulls wheeled overhead; no dolphins sported among the waves. I was a thousand miles from nowhere. Then I remembered I was a vampire: suddenly the sun was roasting me alive! The heat seared me to my core.

I awoke shivering. I was cold. For a moment I didn't know where I was. I felt around with my hands. I was in a box. Then it came back: I lay aboard a freighter. I felt under me: I was still atop the blanket on the mattress. I fumbled around till I found the jacket I had brought. I arranged it on top of me, figuring later to crawl under the covers as needed.

I was thirsty. I remembered the blood bags and reached behind me, found the icebox, and flipped up its lid. My hand groped inside and found a bag floating in cool water. What happened to the ice? Saigon's heat must have worked fast. I opened the bag and sipped on the blood – it tasted bad. Oh, great. Now I'd have nothing to eat for two weeks.

I heard voices and footsteps. My trunk lurched and began to slide along the floor. *What, they need to move me somewhere else?* The trunk crunched to a halt, and once again the electric motor hummed. My crate rose steadily. The motor stopped. The crate sat still. Then I felt myself being lifted awkwardly, and again there was rhythmic swaying. Alarmed, I began to worry. *Where are they taking me? Have I been found out? Has the captain ordered me brought above for a ritual beheading?* This would teach me to catnap.

Now the trunk angled downward and the footfalls rang hollow. *Are they taking me back off the ship? Has there been a mistake? How much trouble am I in?*

My little crypt rattled to a halt. Car doors slammed. The world bounced a bit. An engine churned to life. I sensed the rolling motion of a vehicle.

Now I heard a key in a lock. Hinges creaked; light poured in. Foxtrot was looking down at me. He was dressed differently than when he had locked me into my sleeping box. He said, "How're you feeling?"

I replied, "Is something wrong? How come you took me back off the ship?"

Foxtrot looked puzzled. Then he smiled. "We're here. We're in Long Beach."

My eyes grew wide. *"Where?"*

"Welcome to California."

30

"I must have really blacked out on that ship," I murmured. We were driving north on the freeway toward Santa Monica. Just outside the port, we had transferred to a dark, nondescript sedan driven by another team member. Now I sat in the back, sipping on a blood bag and gazing at the glittering lights of the megalopolis at night.

Next to me, Foxtrot said, "Jager figured you'd fall asleep pretty fast and stay that way. He says it's a vampire thing. You guys get in a crate and just snooze off."

I didn't like it that Jager knew more about me than I did. Normally I awoke right after sunset like clockwork, but something about sea travel had changed the rules. I still had a lot to learn about myself. I resolved to do a better job of visiting libraries here than I had in Saigon. L.A. was a big place with lots of resources. In fact, UCLA was supposed to be fairly close to Santa Monica, and it was known for its huge research libraries.

We exited the freeway on a cloverleaf at Wilshire Boulevard and headed west toward the ocean. After about three miles we turned left, drove a few blocks, and entered a driveway that ramped down beneath a nondescript two-story building. We parked, got out, and Foxtrot and I took the elevator to the second floor. We walked along a hallway; gray carpet muffled our footsteps. The lighting was fluorescent. As always, I could hear the high-pitched scream of the ballasts.

A team member stood near the end of the hall. As we approached, he opened a door. Foxtrot and I stepped through. Inside at a conference table sat Jager. "Join me," he said, waving us to chairs.

The door behind us closed. We sat. As usual, Jager was wearing his reading glasses and scribbling into a notebook. Oddly, the sight of him working made me feel at home, as if nothing had changed, really, except for the minor detail of a new office on a continent halfway around the world.

Jager looked at us. "So, how was the trip?"

Foxtrot and I glanced at each other. I cleared my throat. "Took about five minutes. I slept the whole way."

Jager nodded. "Good. As expected." He bent to his notes, mumbling, "*Jar of soil effective as soporific.*"

I asked, "What, did you put sleeping gas in my crate, or something?"

Jager smiled and shook his head. "Ocean travel can cause a vampire's internal clock to go astray. A jar of earth will soothe the creature's nervous system. Usually, he or she will simply fall asleep and stay that way until the voyage is concluded. In your case, it worked perfectly. I didn't want you wide awake for two weeks, fidgeting inside a box." He turned to Foxtrot. "Report."

"Sir. No problems at all. The crew showed no curiosity about the trunk, and none of the telltales I placed on or near it were disturbed. Beyond that, we had a day of rough seas, but nothing else of interest."

Jager nodded again and made more notes. "Good. Full report on my desk tomorrow noon. Dismissed." Foxtrot rose, nodded to me, and left.

Jager finished writing. "Christian, we have booked rooms for you at a hotel down by the beach. We have transferred your clothing there, and we have placed into your suite the trunk you just used, so you can continue to sleep in it."

I pondered that. "And my blood supply?"

"In your refrigerator. We have left strict instructions that your rooms not be disturbed. As in Saigon, we will take care of cleaning your suite. However, we expect to be here indefinitely, so you may wish eventually to make other living arrangements. I can recommend a realtor."

I was surprised. "You don't care if I live away from the team?"

"America is a big place. If you wanted to run off, you could do so, whether you lived next door to us or not. Besides, I think you deserve to enjoy yourself. You have earned it."

"Oh, stop trying to talk me out of it."

He chuckled. "I should warn you, however, that our resources on this side of the ocean are vastly larger than they were in Saigon. Were you to disappear, we are quite confident we could locate you again."

I clasped my hands behind my head and leaned back. "I don't doubt it. But these 'resources' – do they include other vampires?"

"Perhaps."

"Do you have any vamps besides me who work for you?"

"Perhaps."

"Well, I'd really like to–"

"We will introduce you to our other assets as necessary."

I rolled my eyes. "Yessir, captain sir!"

Jager looked over his glasses at me. "You really don't have to take that tone."

I grinned. "I'm a vampire. I'm supposed to be quirky."

"Yes. Well," and he wrote quickly on a piece of notepaper, "here is the address of the hotel." He handed the paper across the table and gave me directions. He said a driver would be here in about an hour to ferry team members to the hotel, or I could simply walk. "It is about a mile from here, and I am certain you can cover that distance in a minute or so. But please bring your *quirky* self back to this office tomorrow night at eight sharp. We may already have an assignment for you."

I grinned. "Now you're talkin'."

31

On my way back down the hall, I found an open door and poked my head in. The room was dimly lit. A team member sat at a bank of black-and-white TV monitors. Each was trained on a different part of the building we were in, except for a couple aimed at places I didn't recognize. The team member held a pen and made an occasional note on a log sheet. For a few moments I gazed at the monitors. The team member looked up, saw me, and nodded. I smiled and walked out.

Further down the hall was another open door, and again I peeked in. This time, the room was brightly lit. It seemed to be a small kitchen lounge. Delta sat at a table, munching on potato chips. He also watched a TV screen, but this one showed an episode of a Western drama – *Bonanza*, as I recall. Cowboys chased other cowboys on horseback, guns blazing, and now and then a player fell from his horse. Good old American television. I hadn't seen any in years. I watched for a few minutes until Hoss said something cutely inane and his brothers laughed obligingly. I left.

I decided to hoof it to the hotel. I took the elevator to the lobby, but the glass entrance doors were locked. I recalled that one of the monitors upstairs was connected to a camera aimed at the front of the building. The monitor hadn't picked up the lobby interior very well through the reflective sheen of the front glass, so I pressed myself against the doors, my nose smashed flat, and began waving my arms. After about ten seconds, a solenoid buzzed and the door bolt clicked open. I pushed out.

The night air was cool and slightly damp. It was late. I could smell the ocean. I walked to the corner and began loping down the nearly empty boulevard. Though I held myself in check, still I was moving at nearly the speed of an automobile, and I arrived at the hotel in about three minutes.

Inside the lobby, I banged on the desk bell. A concierge

emerged from a back room, rubbing sleep from his eyes. I gave him the name from my latest false ID; he pulled room keys from a slot and handed them to me. He wished me pleasant dreams.

I took the elevator upstairs. My room was at the far end of the corridor. I unlocked the door, stepped inside, and flipped the light switch. The living room was spacious, as nicely done up as my old suite at the Majestic. I walked through to the kitchen and turned on the lights. Covered overhead flourescents flickered to life, bathing the beautiful cabinetry and glossy appliances in a cool light. Very modern. I checked the fridge: blood bags aplenty, stacked neatly on three shelves.

The bedroom and bath were just as nice. In a corner lay my trunk, unlocked. I walked over and lifted the lid. Inside, the made-up mattress was as I had left it hours before, along with the jar of soil. The transit icebox was gone, though, and my heavy jacket lay draped over the end of the queen-sized bed.

I checked the walk-in closet. My Saigon clothes were hung neatly on the rods. A built-in dresser stood at the far end. I opened the top drawer and found my various pairs of dark glasses arranged next to my watches. The other drawers contained sweaters, jeans, and socks, plus neat little piles of tidy whities that I never used.

Everything was in place. I walked back to the living room, went to the window, and pushed the drapes aside with my hand. Below me, maybe twenty yards from the hotel, surf boiled against a floodlit beach. Beyond lay blackness. As I watched, a night bird flickered past.

I was going to like it here.

32

It turned out my first assignment was to study street maps of the Los Angeles area. Jager wanted me to know my way around. He handed me a box filled with map books and sent me to an empty office to study. I felt like one of those English cabbies practicing for the license exam by memorizing every street in London. The work was dull but quick: my vampiric nervous system soaked up entire books filled with detailed maps of L.A., Orange, and Ventura counties; I had the region memorized in a few hours. I then learned the locations of most of the major buildings and points of interest in the area. I'd never been to Southern California before, but now I almost knew the place like a local.

I brought the box back to the conference room – which seemed to double as Jager's office – said, "Done," and walked down the hall to the lounge, where I sat with a couple of team members and watched television.

We were discussing how to approach Jager about getting one of the new color-TV sets when he walked in, carrying another box. He plopped it down on the kitchen table in front of me. "And now, Christian, San Francisco." I stared at the box. It was jammed with more maps.

One team member groaned, "Aw, man, that's tough!" The other shook his head and laughed. Jager gazed at me expectantly.

I asked, "Now?"

"Yes, please."

I shrugged, rose, picked up the heavy box in one hand and, twirling it on my fingers like a basketball, glided out of the room.

I had the Bay Area memorized a couple of hours later. I brought the box back to the conference room. "Anything else?" I asked.

"Yes, San Diego." Jager saw the look on my face. "Er, but tomorrow will be fine. Take the rest of the night off."

By week's end, Jager had gotten me to learn the streets of several more cities, including a few east of California. I began to wonder what sort of travel plans he had in mind for me. Would I be shipped by train to my destinations? By truck?

I got a job the following week. Jager pushed across the desk a piece of paper with a street number in downtown LA. I looked down at it. He handed me a set of car keys. I looked at those, too; they were for a Porsche. "You want me to drive to the location? In a sports car? This is a first."

"I assume you know how to operate a stick shift."

"Well, yeah. I repaired a couple back in high school."

"Excellent. The vehicle is especially adept at high-speed maneuvering, in the event you run into some sort of tail."

"Hell, I could just jog downtown and back. Bet I could outrun a sports car."

"Yes, I imagine you could. However, in Los Angeles, pedestrians are conspicuous while drivers blend in. You will find an automobile highly useful here."

I looked down again at the keys. "So I've heard. Okay, what's the assignment?"

"Your target is a file folder in a small office at the address I have given you on Third Street, just west of the Harbor Freeway. It is run by the Soviet embassy but has no markings. We want you to access some papers that look like these." He handed me sheets covered in typed Cyrillic lettering. I had rarely seen Russian writing, but my mind decrypted the text quickly. I understood that these were personnel files.

New for this job was the type of alarm system – a key-pad that, when an exterior door was opened, threatened to squawk loudly if you didn't quiet it with a code entered into the pad. "It is similar to the number pad on a Princess phone," Jager said. "Have you seen them?"

"Yeah. A friend back home had a sister who used one. It was pink. The keypad lit up when you lifted the handset. You pushed the buttons to dial the phone."

"Exactly. Now, the model you will encounter can be disarmed with this code." He handed me a piece of paper with a six-digit number on it.

I memorized it and handed it back. "How'd you get this info?"

"That is confidential. Suffice it to say we have sources inside the Russian embassy."

Jager then handed me a very small object. "This is a camera. The papers are to be photographed, not stolen. You should try your best to leave no sign of your presence there. We need the information from those papers, but we do not wish to spark an international incident." He showed me how to work the camera. Then he set it down next to the paper with the address and pointed to them both. "Got it?"

The camera was straightforward. The address fit nicely onto my memorized mental map of the downtown L.A. area. "Got it."

"Excellent. We will have team members in position nearby to monitor and provide assistance. However, there is one catch."

"Go on."

"We do not know exactly where the papers are located within the building. You may have to do quite a bit of searching to find them."

I nodded. "Whatever it takes."

"Good. You may leave immediately. Enjoy the car."

I took the elevator to the underground garage. Parked in a dark corner was a black Porsche 911, one of those sexy new machines everyone had been gaga about for the past few years. I'd only heard of them, having been otherwise occupied overseas. Now I had a chance to drive one.

I sat in the leather seat, found the ignition slot, turned the key, and the car roared to life. I released the brake, gave it some gas and let out the clutch. It jerked forward and headed straight for the far wall. Lucky for me, I had extremely fast reflexes, or I wouldn't have hit the brake pedal in time. Chastened, I adjusted my instincts and carefully reversed the car, then drove it up the ramp to the street beyond. I turned right and headed north to Wilshire Boulevard.

Now that I understood the car, it behaved beautifully. I quickly discovered that, on city streets under the speed limit, the Porsche didn't really want to get out of second gear. This beast was meant for the open road.

I found my way to the freeway and took the winding onramp. The car liked curves! This would be fun. Within moments I changed to the Santa Monica Freeway and raced east, heedless of the speed, snaking my way through traffic. This was the most fun I'd had since ... since ... with a shock, I remembered Ai Phuong. My foot came off the gas pedal. I drove the rest of the trip under the speed limit.

I found my way through the eccentric web of exit lanes and frontage roads to Third Street. The office was midway down an unassuming block of buildings, typical of the low-profile places Russians liked to use. I found a parking spot a few blocks away, locked the car, and jogged back to the target in less than a minute.

I jumped onto a nearby roof and surveyed the building. A small stairwell enclosure jutted from the target roof above the second floor. I decided to enter that way. The street was just a bit too wide for me to jump across without making a noisy landing. I dropped to the sidewalk, crossed the road, and leapt onto the building's roof. It was covered in wide strips of that asphalt composite that tended to crunch underfoot, so I took special care to step quietly. The roof entry door lock was a snap, literally. Then I remembered I wasn't supposed to leave evidence of my presence. Oops.

Just inside, I found the electric keypad on the wall, buzzing angrily, a red light blinking. I entered the disarm code Jager had given me. The noisy red light switched to silent green. So far, so good.

I glided noiselessly down the stairs to the second floor. Our intel didn't include a map of the place, so I had to check each room for file cabs. Every space I looked into contained them. I was just beginning to think this would be a lengthy process, and then it got worse: I found the main document room on the first floor, jammed with dozens of metal cabinets. Most of them were locked, some with keyed buttons, some with dials. The dials I outwitted easily, but none held personnel files. For the button locks I had brought a small tool, and I picked a few of the locks. But there must have been thirty such cabinets, and time was short. So I took to pulling each cabinet away from the wall and prying open the rear panel with my fingers. I'd release the latch, open the drawers, check the files, flatten the rear sheet metal the best I could, and finally press the cabinet back against the wall. I hoped the damage would remain hidden for weeks or months. By then the natural paranoia of Soviet security would turn inward, searching for moles.

I couldn't find the papers anywhere. I was about to leave the room and search all the other offices when I noticed a rather large pile of files resting on a desk in the corner. On a hunch, I went to it and flipped through the files. There, toward the bottom, was the one I wanted.

I pulled out the camera and took a snap of every page. Then carefully I replaced the file exactly where it had lain in the pile.

The way out was simple enough. I retraced my steps upstairs to the rooftop door, reset the alarm keypad, opened the roof door, stepped into the cool evening air, and got shot three times point-blank.

33

The bullets smashed into my chest and abdomen, slamming me against the stair house. I bounced off and lay stunned on the gritty asphalt roofing. A silhouette with a gun spoke Russian into a walkie-talkie. A staticky voice answered. My ears could hear the same voice from the street below. Apparently they had posted guards at all the exits, and the roof guy had made the hit. From the chatter, I gathered that the rest of their team was heading our way. This was going badly. Jager would not be amused.

Two of the bullets had passed clean through me. I glanced over and saw the small holes in the wall. One of the bullets had bounced around inside my gut, causing God knows what damage to my corpse's innards. But I had no time. I rose to my feet. Already the wounds were healing. I heard a plop as the third bullet worked its way out of the front of my stomach and dropped onto the roof. The silhouetted man turned, saw me standing, and raised his silenced pistol toward me once more. But I leapt forward, twisted the gun from his grip, and struck a blow on his chin that whipped his head around and snapped his neck. His body crumpled in a heap.

It was too late to hide evidence, so I left the body there and, at a full run, jumped up and across the street to the next building. I landed just barely on the edge of its roof, teetering over the street for a moment before catching my balance. I looked back; the other Russian team members were spilling out onto their roof. Two of them ran to the body of their comrade while the others scanned the area. One caught sight of me as I turned to go. He fired his weapon. I could hear bullets zing past my ears as I escaped.

I leapt to the next roof, and the next. As I ran, I heard more gunshots behind me. I wondered if our team had engaged the Russians, but I had no time to double back and investigate. I jumped down to the street and raced to my car.

When I got there, I found a young man trying to pry open the door with a jimmy. I materialized next to him. He looked up at me with a start. "Jeez! Where'd you come from?" he asked.

"This is my car."

"Hey, it belongs to whoever found it. But we can always work together. You take the tires, I'll take the radio and the gauges."

I glared at him. "I mean, I *own* this car. I parked it here."

He stared at me a moment. Then he struck me hard in the face with the metal jimmy. That smarted. I picked him up by the neck until he dangled above me, gagging and clutching at my hand. "Go steal something else," I snarled, and threw him against a nearby wall. He tumbled to the sidewalk and lay motionless. Blood began to pool beneath his head. The blood gave me an intense desire to walk over and, I dunno, see if he had any left. But I thought better of it.

I climbed into the car and began to drive away. At the end of the block just ahead, a gray sedan skidded around the corner and headed straight for me. My vampire's eyes could just make out a couple of faces through the windshield above the bright headlights. They looked like the men I had seen on the rooftop. I braked, slammed my car into reverse, and backed up at about fifty miles an hour down the street. At the next corner I spun the sports car into a bootleg turn, shifted to second, and blasted off into the night.

The gray sedan followed, gaining on me. I floored it and the car's engine howled, pressing me into the seat. I headed west to Vermont Avenue, where I roared left through a red light, barely missing a hobo walking across the street, and sped south.

I looked in the mirror. In moments, a pair of lights wobbled into view, steadied, and began to widen. They were gaining on me again! That was some kind of souped-up vehicle they had. I gunned it, racing along Vermont as it rolled up and down on the uneven geography. I ignored stoplights, relying on my reaction time and the excellent car to get me through. Also, it helped that there was very little traffic at two in the morning.

As I drove, I wondered, *How did they know I was there?*

Did I trip a silent alarm? Then my suspicious side wondered if I had been set up.

But I had no time to ponder. Behind me I heard a siren. In the mirror I saw a steady red light above a set of headlights. I sighed with relief. I guessed I could outrun him while his patrol car ran cover between me and the Russkies.

Ahead loomed the freeway overpass. I skidded right and up the onramp. The police car followed. I couldn't tell if the Russians were still behind us.

I raced along the frontage lanes until a gap in the divider appeared. I barreled onto the main portion of Interstate 10, heading west toward the ocean. In moments I had the Porsche screaming along at about 140. The cop car couldn't keep up; its lights narrowed to a tiny point.

I had just breathed a sigh of relief when I saw two more sets of lights behind me. Both were gaining. One had a red light off to the side. The other must have been the Russian guys, though they lurked well behind the red-light car. The city police couldn't keep up with me, but the Russians and this vehicle were doing just fine. I wondered who was driving the new one. Then I recalled, while doing map study, some Auto Club brochures that had sung the praises of the highly skilled officers of the California Highway Patrol, whose beat included the freeways. So the pros had been called in. I accelerated once more, this time pinning the needle on the speedometer. Our little caravan zoomed through the 405 interchange. The freeway, I knew from the maps, would empty out onto the coast road in a few miles. In less than two minutes, I would have to make a decision.

The Lincoln exit was fast approaching. I worked my way into the left lanes; the Highway Patrol cruiser followed about two lengths behind. Further back, the Russians in the gray sedan gave chase. At the last possible moment I swerved violently to the right, just making it onto the Lincoln ramp. The patrol car was large and powerful, but it simply couldn't corner like the Porsche, and it blazed off down the freeway, out of the game. But the Russians had time to adjust, and they followed me up the ramp.

I careened right at Lincoln and hurtled along the street. We weren't far from Jager's office, but I had no intention of going there. Instead I sped north. I was beginning to realize that these guys weren't going to get lost. So I decided it was time to be a vampire.

34

At the top of Lincoln, I dog-legged through a posh residential area and swerved down the curving road into Santa Monica Canyon. The Russkies were close behind. Idly I thought, *I really want a look at that car's engine!* I wasn't disappointed at all in the performance of my little 911. But somehow it had met its match. Tonight I would have to rely on powers of a non-mechanical sort.

The canyon road emptied onto the Pacific Coast Highway, where I swerved right and dashed north. After about a mile I saw what I wanted, a large lot on the ocean side of the road, meant for the parked cars of sunbathing tourists. At an intersection, I swung across and onto the lot, driving to the far end and spinning around to face my pursuers. I put the high beams on – I wanted my pursuers as blinded as possible – shut off the engine, and stepped out.

The gray sedan pulled up and stopped about twenty yards away. I waited. Nothing happened for a few moments. Then the doors opened and three burly men piled out.

They advanced on me slowly, guns drawn. The lead man held up a hand and they halted. He said in a thick accent, "You steal from us. Please to give back."

I shrugged. "Hey, I couldn't find a damn thing worth taking! I was looking for cash, but all you guys got is papers and desks."

The Russians glanced at each other. The leader said, "You are *schpione!* You spy for Americans. Give us what you steal. And we will let you go."

One of the men behind him sniggered. The leader shot him a look. I said, "Guys, guys! The chase was fun, but really I didn't take anything."

The leader sneered at me, then turned to the men and spoke quickly in Russian. I heard the word "*Smert*" – death – so I knew they meant to start shooting. The man to the leader's right raised his silenced weapon and fired.

But I was already standing at his side. I yanked the gun away and slugged him hard in the chest. My fist crushed his sternum and flattened his ribs, pulping his heart. He dropped off my hand and hit the pavement. I stepped over to the leader, grabbed him by the hair, and pulled his head sharply down against my upturned knee, smashing his face. I lifted his head and checked: the nose was punched inward, the nasal bones shoved into his brain. I figured he'd be dead within a minute.

I let him drop and turned to the third Russian. About a second and a half had passed since the first gunman had fired his weapon. The third man only had time to gape. I grabbed his shoulders, pulled him to me, and enjoyed a light dessert of blood from his neck. Oh my God, it was lip-smacking good. I'd missed that taste.

As usual, I stopped before I went too far. I pulled back and looked down at him. He was still conscious, staring groggily up at me. He mumbled something like, *"Vampeer!"* Then I remembered he was speaking Russian.

"Yes, I'm a *vampeer*," I leered, "and you three screwed with the wrong dead guy!" I broke his neck.

Quickly I went to the car and looked inside. I found a camera in the glove compartment. I opened it and unreeled the film, exposing it to the light from the street lamp. Then carefully I wound the acetate back into the camera and left it on the floor, its back slightly ajar. I stuffed the three dead men into the car. I walked out to the beach, took off my shoes, and packed them with sand. I brought the shoes back to the gray sedan and poured the sand onto the bloody pavement, spreading it out with my foot until all signs of struggle had been covered. I fussed with my shoes and socks for a moment, making sure all the extra sand grains were removed – I didn't want to wear grit – and put them back on.

I leaned into the sedan and pulled the hood lever, then raised the hood. The engine was huge, a 442 or something like it, probably bored out even bigger. No wonder they'd been up my rear. I slammed the hood shut, climbed into the driver's seat, and drove slowly and carefully – no need to meet any more policemen tonight – back down the Pacific Coast Highway. I turned onto the incline that led up to Santa

112

Monica, made my way past the cliffside park, and took the short bridge down onto the city pier. I drove past the carousel to a large empty area away from the tourist shops. I stopped near the edge of the pier, got out, moved the chief Russian's body into the driver's seat, put the car in gear, and shut the door. The car began to roll forward. With my foot I gave it a shove; it was doing maybe thirty miles an hour when it sailed off the pier. I blurred to the edge and looked down in time to see the sedan hit the water with a great splash. The car bobbed for a moment, flipped over, and disappeared.

I was feeling good. Tonight I had photographed enemy documents, evaded assailants and the police, killed three men, destroyed evidence, and treated myself to a little fresh human blood. I must have broken dozens of laws tonight, *and* gotten away with my first vampire kill in America. All of it made me feel ... jaunty.

That, and my new car was awesome.

I jogged back along the beach to the lot. The Porsche was parked where I had left it. I walked to the back end, bent down, and used my fingers to remove the bolts that attached the license plate to the rear bumper. I pulled the plate, tossed it on the passenger seat, got in, and drove back to the office.

35

I sat in the conference room, the license plate and camera lying on the table. Foxtrot walked in. Jager spoke quietly to him. Foxtrot nodded and left.

Jager said, "We were set up."

I said, "Do tell."

He said, "One of our team was wounded in the shooting."

I sat up. "Is he okay?"

"Kappa was hit in the upper thigh. He'll recover nicely. With some effort, he should be able to rejoin the team in several weeks."

"I heard shooting after I got away. I wondered."

"Yes, well, when you were shot, the team ran to assault positions, but by the time they were in place, you had already dispatched your assailant and left the area. The Russian team, I am told, fired on you as you escaped, at which point one of our men opened up on them. He missed, but unfortunately they did not. By the time our team got to him and assessed his situation, you and the Russians were long gone."

I nodded. "The car did great, by the way. You should give it a ribbon or something."

"Good. Meanwhile, our source at the Russian embassy has become a liability. We may need to terminate our relationship with him."

I raised my hand. "I volunteer."

Jager smiled. "You will be informed if and when that eventuality arises." He picked up the license plate and dropped it into a box. "We are replacing these on your car as we speak. Good work, by the way, cleaning up the scene afterwards. We have men heading for the beach parking lot to make sure everything is completely spotless." Jager picked up the camera; it disappeared into a desk drawer. "I will have the film developed shortly. For now, we will need you to lay low until we have checked all our intel, to be sure no one else witnessed any of the events of this evening. You are an asset we do not wish to compromise."

That sounded nice. "So I'm on leave."

"More or less. Take the next few days off. Report back here on Monday." He thought for a moment. "You might wish to use this free time to investigate more permanent living arrangements."

I raised an eyebrow. "We're really gonna be here a long time, then."

Jager made some notes. "Yes." I sat there a moment; he ignored me and went on writing. I realized I had been dismissed. I rose and walked out, took the elevator down to my car – the plates were new, the numbers completely different – and drove at a legal pace back to the hotel, where I enjoyed a hot bath and a much-deserved sleep inside my dark little sepulcher of a trunk.

36

I found a small house in Pacific Palisades, not far from a cliff overlooking the ocean. The neighborhood was quiet, low-key and elegant. The house itself was a '50s modernist Ranch set edge-on to the street, the garage and a breezeway in front. I'd been saving my lavish pay and most of the cash I'd stolen: I had enough money in the bank to make the down payment, and then some, without touching my price-less little Swiss-bank collection of filched baubles. The escrow was short, and Jager kept me off duty for weeks, so I spent the time ordering furniture, carpeting, lighting, new plumbing, and front landscaping.

I hired an excavation contractor who still did a side business installing fallout shelters for the hopelessly right wing. I told him, "Those Rooskies are dangerous bastards, I don't trust 'em far enough to spit," and his workers dug up the backyard and installed a very nice bomb shelter with a plastic lining that surrounded the reinforced concrete to keep out moisture. Then I had the landscaper cover it with dichon-dra and flowerbeds.

The evening after escrow closed, the furniture arrived and I moved in. For the first time, I owned a house, and already it was full of stuff. The walls were still bare, though. The next evening I toured the art galleries of the Palisades, Westwood, and Beverly Hills. I liked the Modernists, and I found an early Warhol, a beautifully abstract Ellsworth Kelly, a small work by Pollock, and a Lichtenstein that had a comic-book heroine who reminded me vaguely of Ai Phuong. The art I didn't steal cost almost half as much as the house itself. I installed an alarm system.

The bomb shelter was especially comfy and quiet. I put my travel trunk in there and continued to sleep in it. I could have dropped a mattress on the floor, but the enclosing walls of the trunk made me feel safe. Maybe it's a vampire thing. I don't know.

I was beginning to enjoy my forced idleness, reading several books a day and tooling around the Westside at night. There were lots of bars and clubs where I could meet people, though at first I was mildly bemused that everyone, men and women, now wore their hair long. I kept an eye out for one person in particular, but of course she never showed.

Early one evening, Jager called me in. Big announcement, he said.

I drove the Porsche down to the office and found my way to the conference room. Most of the team was present, crowded into seats or standing next to walls. Jager sat at one end of the table. I slipped through the door and found a place on a wall.

Jager noticed me, set down his glasses, and looked around the room. "We are beginning a new phase of our work. We have received a number of assignments that involve terminations with extreme prejudice. I will be assigning you to squads, and each squad will concentrate on its own series of jobs. You will work closely with the same men over and over, so your skills should meld nicely, which will reduce the chance of error and accident. The exception is Christian, who will be on roving detail as needed."

A couple of the team members glanced up at me. I winked at them.

"There will also, of course, be the usual assortment of break-ins. Our client list has expanded, so we may be hiring before long. You will all have plenty to do. If anyone has a concern about the nature of our new assignments, I understand. Please see me afterward."

I noticed that nobody chatted with the boss when the meeting ended.

And thus began one of the most entertaining phases of my work with Jager.

At first, he kept me busy with the usual stuff – cracking safes, stealing files from desktops, and, after a while, following and photographing people. I worked with a squad that would run cover while I did the breaking and entering. Many of these jobs were like detective work, except instead of following husbands having affairs, I was tracking diplo-

117

mats and foreign military attaches and other people we thought might be spying for the enemy. I was especially good at getting into houses when people were home, rummaging through their closets and desks while they sat in another room having dinner or watching TV. (Once, I snuck into a bedroom occupied by a couple performing rather vigorous sex. I grabbed the target item from the closet, stole money from the couple's wallets – I wondered if they'd blame each other – and snuck back out while they thrashed and moaned.) Some of the photos I made showed people snoring away in bed or taking a shower. A few pics displayed world-famous personalities sitting on the crapper. I got a kick out of those, but Jager told me to cut it out.

Even more fun, though, were the assassinations. During this entire period, which lasted several years, I was personally involved in the death or disappearance of a number of well-known people. I learned how to use the railroads to get around the country when assignments were too far for driving. I took to wearing a special suit that protected me from the sun when the job had to be done during the day. But it was awkward to use and I hated it, so we tried to schedule events for the evenings.

Do you recall George Lincoln Rockwell? A raging neo-Nazi. I was the guy who shot him from a roof, then jumped down and ran off. We pinned it on one of Rockwell's aides, a guy named Patler – naturally we called him *Patsy* – and he did heavy time.

How about Jimmy Hoffa? He was the mob-connected boss of the Teamsters Union. He disappeared. I helped.

Robert Kennedy was a shoe-in for the Democratic nomination for president when I was told to stalk him with malice. As it happened, I had nothing to do with his death. I was standing in the kitchen of the Ambassador Hotel in Los Angeles when somebody else fired the shots. I've never been convinced the killer was Sirhan Sirhan, but I was looking away at that moment, so maybe I'll never know. But clearly there was more than one group trying to get to Kennedy that night.

I *can* tell you that James Earl Ray didn't kill Martin Luther King. I didn't do it either. But I know who did.

Speaking of Kennedys, I managed to learn who killed Robert's brother John. To make a long story short: if you get elected president with the help of the Mob, for Pete's sake don't try to have them all arrested later. That's a really poor idea.

I won't argue that all the wet work we did was noble. But I'm a vampire, and I didn't really care. To me, it was just feuds between different gangs, and I was a hired arbitrator.

I ventured overseas by ship more than once. I traveled to the Middle East around the time Egyptian President Nasser suddenly had a "heart attack" and died. (Let's just say he was delicious.)

Another time, I visited Chile during the period when Marxist Salvador Allende was about to become president. Chilean army Commander-in-Chief Rene Schneider didn't like Allende any better than the rest of the right wing down there, but he took the rather noble stance that the constitution must be obeyed and Allende inaugurated. Unfortunately his decision ran counter to our favorite client's interests. I was sent there to make sure he was taken out of the equation. A Chilean hit squad shot Schneider, but they screwed up the job and he lived. So I visited him in the hospital, and that was that.

A few years later, I was called back to Chile when the same client engineered the coup that finally deposed Allende. Reports allege that, cornered, he committed suicide. But it's more accurate to say that I, ahem, had him for lunch. We didn't want the Schneider snafu to get repeated. That would have been embarrassing.

Speaking of embarrassments, brutal Haitian president Papa Doc Duvalier was a major source of awkwardness for our chief client, and I was sent there in 1971 to hasten his departure from this veil of tears. It didn't take much: he wasn't long for the world in any case. Strangely, when I leaned over his deathbed, he raised his arms to me, intoning, *"Portez-moi au ciel!"* His addled brain must have confused me with an angel.

Abeid Karume ran Zanzibar for about a decade, marginalizing the local Marxists. This should have been enough for our client. But somehow Karume ticked them off, so I took my jar of dirt and sailed around the Cape of Good Hope, landed at Zanzibar Port, and found my way to a card game frequented by Karume, where I watched a small group of men shoot him to death. I didn't need to add my skills to the killing – these guys could teach the Chileans a thing or two – but in the confusion I managed to steal all the money on the card table. It was a tidy sum, which I used to buy a beautiful African art piece that I still own. It's in one of my houses. I forget which.

37

After a couple of years, I had begun to wonder where all the other vampires were. I asked Jager, but he finally confessed that each time the team had encountered a vamp, they had ended up killing it. I was the only exception. Jager suspected other groups, especially the Russians, might also have vampires "on staff." But he couldn't be sure.

I kept my eyes and ears open, especially at watering holes around L.A., watching for telltale signs that someone might be a vampire. I even visited literature groups that specialized in horror, hoping someone might claim to have met a real monster. When Ann Rice's books hit the shelves, the chatter exploded, and vampire clubs started up. But I never met anyone who really knew anything.

I never forgot Ai Phuong, of course. Always I hoped I'd find her, even if that meant the risk of exposing us to the wrath of Jager's team. I wondered how she was doing. Was she still in America? Did she have a lover? A couple of times I thought I caught sight of her in the distance. But when I looked again, she was never there.

Once, though, I actually met another vampire. I had slipped inside a bank vault in Westwood, a few miles east of where I lived. It was late on a winter afternoon, and the sun had set just before I arrived at closing time. The tellers were busy with last-minute customers, and I was a speedy little vampire. The vault door sealed shut and the timer locked me in for the night. I set about my task, which was to open a certain safe-deposit box and retrieve the contents so that Jager could use it to blackmail the owner, who happened to be a dangerous enemy of one of our private clients.

The task went smoothly and I had the rest of the night to poke around in other people's boxes. Within thirty minutes I'd snatched wads of cash, handfuls of diamonds, miscellaneous gems, and a couple of piles of bearer bonds that hadn't yet expired. This was the best haul in a long time. I had the presence of mind to lift only a portion of the loose wealth from any one box. I didn't want the renters to notice right away that they'd been fleeced, or they'd run howling to the bank staff, who might then alert other banks. Then this nice new method of thievery would become more difficult.

I wrapped everything – the target haul plus the little side jobs – neatly into the waist sack I still used from my Saigon days. I settled into a corner for a snooze until morning. But then I heard a bump. I stood, listening, and heard it again. It seemed to come from one of the large boxes on a bottom row. I walked over to investigate. Now, usually I don't scare because most of the time I'm the scariest thing in my neighborhood. But I nearly jumped with fright when the box began to move outward by itself. I stood rigid, watching as a person slowly unfolded himself and stepped out of the box.

He was tall and rather skinny, with dark hair, a long beak of a nose, and a prominent Adam's apple. The guy looked like Ichabod Crane. He stretched and glanced around. When he got to me, he jumped back, as scared as I was.

"What are you doing here?" we both asked at once. We began circling each other warily. I saw his eyes widen about the same time mine did, as we both noticed something we had in common. We were both vampires.

"Uh, this is mighty awkward," he said. "Are you ... are you robbin' the place? 'Cause that's what I was plannin' to do."

"Oh," I said, and relaxed a little. "Well, yeah, I've been through some of the boxes, but I've already got more than I can handle. I didn't get to that wall over there." I pointed. "Feel free."

He watched me, guarded. "Uh, thanks." Suddenly he stuck out his hand. "I'm Henry. But you can call me Hank."

"Christian," I answered, and shook his hand. "This is sort of strange. I don't meet one of my kind everyday."

"Me neither," said Hank. "And I've been around awhile."

"Hank's kind of an old-fashioned name. No offense," I said.

"Yeah. Been suckin' blood since aught-eight. Born in eighteen and eighty-seven." He had an accent I couldn't quite place, but it reminded me of farmers in movie Westerns.

"So you're in your nineties by now," I said.

"Yep. How 'bout you?"

"Not quite that old," I said. I wasn't sure how powerful an old vampire might be, so I didn't want to let on. Ai Phuong had been only a few years older than me as a vampire, and much smaller, but she had overpowered me more than once.

"Well, I s'pose we're stuck with each other tonight," he said, smiling awkwardly. "So if ye don' mind, I'll jes' get to work here..." and he indicated the virgin wall of safe-deposit boxes.

"Sure, go ahead. Be my guest." I retreated to my corner of the vault, sat on the linoleum, and watched as Hank made quick work of the entire wall. Like me, he only took a few items from each box. Apparently he was as cautious as I was. His fingers were remarkably deft – much swifter than mine – and before long he had a pile of pelf dumped in one corner. From watching him steal, I picked up a couple of tricks that I figured would help me on future heists. He had an efficient way of using one hand to work open a new box while the other sorted and removed items from the previous box. He got through entire rows in several minutes.

Soon he was done. He had his own cloth bag for stashing loot, and it was jammed.

I asked, "How are you gonna get that thing out of here? It's kind of hard to hide."

Hank looked over at me. "Same as you, I reckon. Just move fast when they ain't lookin'." He shrugged and turned up his hands, as if to say, "How else?"

I nodded. "What were you doing inside that box? Living there?"

He chuckled. "Naw. I did a little reconnoitering early this mornin', decided to peep inside when the bank opened, before it got too light out, an' discovered a few big empty boxes. So I decided to stay inside one and catch some shuteye while I waited for closin' time."

We sat in our respective corners for a couple of hours, doing nothing. I don't fidget, and neither did he.

Eventually I asked, "So how come you haven't tried to attack me and take my stuff?"

He looked up, surprised. "Say again?"

"How come we haven't fought?"

"What, you wanna fight?"

"Not particularly. But I thought ... I just thought vampires were violent and dangerous."

He looked at me quizzically. "Well, sure they're violent – to live humans. But not to each other. Leastways, not so as I've seen."

"Really." I paused. "So, you've met other vampires?"

"Oh, sure. A few times. 'Course'n there was the one who made me. But he was a decent sort. Very helpful getting me started and all." He adjusted himself against the wall. "The other ones I met were jes' as ordinary as pie. Besides – no sense pickin' a fight with someone as strong as you are."

"That's true. But the one I met, she was pretty wild."

His ears perked up. "*She?* Well, that's differnt!" He peered at me. "Yep, I can see it. You were in love. No surprise it was wild."

I leaned back and picked at a small scuffmark on the floor. "So, you've been stealing from vaults for a while now?"

"Oh, off and on fer a few decades. By now I've got plenty, most of it stashed in places around the country, includin' a few safety boxes o' my own. Fact is, I don' really need to steal no more. I jes' like to do it for the fun of it. For the practice."

"Huh."

"Bought a coupla homes, too. But I like to travel. I tend to live outta hotels mostly."

"And you hunt people?"

"Oh, of course. I prefer hobos and vagabonds and small-time crooks, on account of they're not likely to be missed. Don' wanna attract too much attention. What's more, in recent years I notice I don' need much blood a-tall. I kin go fer days, sometimes weeks, without huntin'."

"Then you have no problem resisting temptation, so to speak, when you need to lay low?"

"When I was a young-un, I had a terrible thirst. But now

124

I kin take it or leave it, most days."

I thought about that. "Is there a way you can be reached? Because I might have an interesting project for you."

He raised an eyebrow. "You mean, workin' fer ya?"

"Well, not me, exactly. But I could get you in."

"Reg'lar human bein's? Not vampires?"

"Except for me. They know how to handle our kind, and they've killed a few of us. But if you can keep your fangs to yourself, they're easy to get along with. And the work is very entertaining."

"Hmm. I dunno ... hadn't thought of teamin' up. I'm a bit of a loner. But I must confess I'm curious." He was silent a moment. "Well, you can always contact me at my postal box in Missouri." He pronounced it *Mizzoorah*. He rattled off a number and an address.

I nodded. "Got it. I'll let you know if something comes up."

"I don' usually get nothin' personal there, but since you might send me somethin', I'll make a point of checkin' it more often."

"You'll travel all the way to Missouri just to pick up some mail? That's a bit of a trip."

He grinned. "Oh, it's nothin'. Why, I've got meself clear acrost the country in a single evenin' a few times. So Missouri is just a hop, skip and a jump."

I laughed. "Oh, come on! You're yanking my chain."

"No, I swan! You should try it. It's do-able. You'll feel purty proud o' yerself."

Either this guy was a natural down-home country spinner of tall tales, or I had yet more to learn about my own abilities. True, I had chased Ai Phuong all over Saigon, and at the time I was vaguely aware that we were moving much faster than the speediest cars. But I'd never thought to really test myself.

As dawn approached, Hank said, "The biggest risk here is that they're late opening the vault. Then you gotta run for cover from the sun." He lashed his swag bag onto his back, spidered up the wall, and clung to the ceiling in a corner. I stared at him. He said, "Hurry! The door will open in a few seconds. But don' worry. They never look up." I copied him, tying my bag to my waist, placing my hands on two walls where they met, and shimmying up into a dark corner in the rear of the vault.

The huge door opened right on schedule. An assistant manager walked in, made a note on a clipboard, and walked out. Hank dropped to the floor and whisked out through the opening. I followed close on his heels as he zigzagged through the back areas of the bank and out the rear door. Across the street stood the team van. I knocked, and they hustled me inside and drove me straight to my house.

The sun was just peeking through the trees as I dove down into my bomb shelter and twirled the wheel that sealed the door as tight as a submarine. It had been an interesting night, but I was ready for sleep.

38

I dumped the bag's contents onto the conference-room table. I reached down, separated the target items, and pushed them to one side.

Jager leaned across and examined the take. "It appears as if you obtained rather more valuables than could possibly have been within the one box." He thought a moment. "I am not certain that this is, how shall we say, *kosher*."

"I only took one or two things from each box. Just a few rows. I figure they won't notice the loss for weeks or months. Or years."

Jager picked up a loose diamond. He reached back into his desk and pulled out a loupe. He examined the gem for a few seconds, then did the same with several others. He picked up a stack of bonds, riffled through it, and tossed it back. "Interesting."

I said, "Each thing by itself isn't worth a fortune, but together they add up."

"Yes, so I notice." Jager sat back, tapping his teeth with a thumbnail. "This gives me an idea."

"Great minds think alike."

"This could become a side job of sorts for you. We could ... split the take, with half going into the team coffers. I would need to invent a few fictitious clients and have the proceeds move through our accounting system that way. We could then afford to purchase the latest, most advanced equipment and outbid our competition. We would not be as dependent upon our main American benefactor as before."

"On the other hand, why don't I just go around stealing from vaults and keep everything for myself?"

"Well, you can, of course, on your own time. But you would not have the benefit of our intelligence gathering. We could point you toward vulnerable bank vaults, help plan your ingress, and drive you away afterward."

"That's true. So, do you want half of this?" I pointed at

the table.

Jager waved at it dismissively. "Take it. We can split the next haul. You did well to think of it and to bring it to me. I appreciate your honesty."

"And now we're gonna be dishonest all over town."

"Well, it is the way we do business. This new activity would merely *extend* our skill sets into new areas."

I put my hands on my hips. "So I'm Robin Hood, right?"

Jager chuckled. "Stealing from the rich and giving to the vampire."

I dropped my hands and sighed. "There's absolutely no way to justify this morally. I mean, I don't care if I'm a bad guy, but I liked the idea that the rest of you are basically on the side of good."

Jager folded his hands. "I'm flattered. If it helps, I will point out that our work is part of a worldwide effort to stop Communism and other assaults on our way of life. The government taxes its citizens to pay for that war. A little extra help in the form of baubles from the wealthy cannot hurt the campaign."

"And you really believe that."

Jager pursed his lips. "I suppose ... one could make the argument."

I let a few seconds pass. "By the way, I met a vampire."

Jager sat up. "You did?"

"Yes. He was already inside the vault when I got there." I told him about Hank.

Jager's head bobbed up and down several times. "Well, that explains it. Your backup team reported that a second individual exited the bank at the same time as you this morning." Jager mulled it over. "Perhaps we can meet with him."

"I should be there."

"Yes. We can find a neutral spot. With you in place, we would not have to go through the process of incapacitating him."

I shrugged. "This is all new territory. But it might be worth the risk."

39

We contacted Hank by mail. It took a couple of weeks for a reply. He agreed to meet us at a park in Venice, just south of Santa Monica. We were in place at midnight when we heard ringing from a nearby phone booth. Jager answered it. He spoke for a few moments, then hung up.

He walked back to me. "Hank is nearby, and he described for me the location of each of our hidden team members and their equipment. He says he'll talk to you and me only." Jager made some hand signals; I saw movement in the bushes around the park, and men appeared from the shadows and walked back to the van.

It was quiet. Nothing happened for about five minutes. Then Hank appeared suddenly, standing next to us. "Howdy," he said.

I shook his hand. "Thanks for coming."

Hank said, "Not sure I like all the secret-agent stuff, Mister—"

"Jager," said Jager, and held out his hand.

"Don't," I said, grabbing Hank's arm. "These guys are tricky."

Jager shot a look at me. I continued, "Hank, they can take down a vampire pretty easily. You got the jump on them tonight, but eventually they'd figure out how to out-smart you. As long as you understand how dangerous they are, and you respect them for it, I think they'll be willing to treat you as a normal team member. Right, Jager?"

Jager looked at us both. "Christian is correct. And I trust him or I would not be here. If you can give us the benefit of the doubt, Hank, I think we can do the same for you."

Hank shrugged. "Seems fair. I'm here 'cause Christian tells me you-all got some innerestin' work for me to do."

Jager smiled. "That, we do. Indeed, we do."

From there, things went better than I'd expected. Hank agreed, as a contract worker for Jager, to suspend his hunt for human blood. "Like I said, lately I don' much care 'bout it one way or t'other," he explained. Hank took over the suite I'd abandoned at the hotel. I showed him how to heat blood from the bags Jager provided, should he need the sustenance. He quickly became an avid member of the team, and Jager was able to double the number of jobs that required the skills of a vampire. Hank proved to be honest and stable, and within weeks he was a regular presence at the office.

He pulled me aside one evening. "Christian, I gotta thank ya. This is more fun than I've had in years."

I said, "Sure, Hank. I'm glad it worked out so well."

A week later, Jager did the same thing. "Christian, I must thank you for bringing Hank to my attention. Aside from you, I had despaired of finding a vampire who was able to integrate with humans in a group effort. But he seems to have risen to the challenge admirably."

I said, "I had an instinct about him. So far, it looks like I guessed right."

With Hank on the team, Jager was able to plan several bank-vault heists. Jager offered some of them to Hank, but he begged off. "Mister, I'm havin' so much fun playing spy that I'd kinda like to continue with that work, if that's all right with you." So I took the bank jobs.

I got very good at entering vaults, sometimes using the Hank method of sleeping inside a big deposit box until nightfall, and sometimes simply darting in just before closing. Jager tried to coordinate these little raids with some actual client work. This meant that sometimes I first had to find a target box and remove whatever items our client required. Then I could spend a leisurely evening pilfering the rest of the boxes.

Within months I had doubled my wealth. The Swiss bankers who carefully stored the items I sent them stayed honest, as far as I could tell. Occasionally I would run a spot check on them, requesting that they return to me one of the boxes, and each time it would appear within days by special delivery, the seals still on it, everything inside untouched.

Later I would be glad Hank had refused these jobs, because the wealth it gave me would come in handy when Jager had his heart attack.

40

Jager's health had been deteriorating for some time. Though he never smoked in front of the men, I knew he had a pack-a-day habit. He was overweight and his skin looked ashen. Finally, a dozen years into our California adventure, Jager suffered a massive coronary.

I got to the hospital that evening. Jager was just coming out of surgery. Delta and another team member stood in the waiting room talking to the surgeon. He was saying, "...And we completed a quadruple bypass. But his heart suffered a lot of damage. He's not out of the woods. But we're hopeful." We were told not to bother waiting, as he would be allowed no visitors until tomorrow at the earliest. Delta dismissed the other team member, found a chair, and took up a post at the entrance to the intensive-care unit. I stayed, too, and wandered the halls.

I walked passed the blood depository, backed up, and snuck inside. I stole a bag of O-positive and slurped it down. It was cold and bland, but I needed it. It steadied my nerves.

A little after midnight, I ghosted back to the I.C. unit, nodded to Delta, and eased over to where Jager lay. His face was obscured by an oxygen mask. I looked down at him, my thoughts a muddle. What if he died? What would happen to the team? What, for that matter, would happen to me? I had more than enough money to live like a prince forever, but without Jager's work I wouldn't know what to do with myself.

Jager's eyes fluttered open. Groggily he focused, looked around, and found me. He pulled the mask from his face. "Where am I?"

"Saint John's I-C-U. You had a heart attack. They gave you a bypass. I'm not supposed to be here."

"What time is it?"

"After midnight."

"What day?"

"Well, you had your heart attack yesterday afternoon."

"Oh. I see." He rested awhile. Then: "If I don't make it..."

"I can fix that. You can become like me."

Jager's eyes got big. "No. No. That is not a good idea."

"Why not?"

Jager rested some more. "I appreciate the offer. But it ... it is just not for me."

I shrugged. "Say the word and it's yours."

Tears popped out of his eyes. That was unexpected. "Really, thank you. But no."

I said, "You should rest."

His hand shot out and grabbed my wrist. "Not yet. There is something you must do."

"What do you need?"

"If I die, you have to take over the company."

I never could get over his capacity to surprise me. "Me? Why me?"

"Because you love this company as much as I do. You do not understand how it operates, but you want the work to go on."

"I like working for *you*. But it's just a business."

"Do not delude yourself. I strongly suspect you identify more with this work than with being a vampire."

I folded my arms. "Where do you get all this?"

Jager breathed for a while. "I am good at reading people. Anyway, I trust you more than anyone to take care of things. There are some papers in the vault behind my desk in the conference room. Bring them to me. There is not much time."

"The doc says you're gonna be okay."

"The doc is wrong."

"How do you know?"

"I just know. Now go and get those papers."

I drove to the office, found the items I was looking for, and brought them back to the hospital. At the I.C.U. door, I told Delta I'd take over till morning. He nodded and stood. He glanced in at Jager's sleeping form, then turned back to me. Delta's eyes looked haunted. He turned and walked toward the elevators.

132

I went to Jager's bedside. He was asleep. I didn't want to wake him. I went out and sat in Delta's guard chair.

After an hour, his voice rasped, "Do you have the papers?"

I rose and walked in. "Yes."

"Good. I am transferring control of the company to you. But it would be better if you bought it outright. I think you can afford it by now."

My jaw dropped; my fangs must have showed.

"The agreement will include an escrow, so you will have time to obtain the funds you need from your Swiss resources."

Again I asked, "Why me?"

"Like I said, I trust you to keep this enterprise going."

At that moment, I knew he was right. I *did* want the company to continue. But I didn't want to be Jager. I didn't want to run it. I wanted to play inside it.

"I'm not a manager," I told him. "I wouldn't know how to run a business if I tried."

Jager managed a small smile. "I know. That is why I want you to rely on Delta and Foxtrot. They know how the levers work and where the bodies are buried. And they can act as the face of the company so you can remain in the background."

I stood there a moment. Then I nodded. "Okay. Okay. Understood."

I reached over and raised the head of his bed higher so he could work. Jager shuffled through the papers. He looked up, frustrated. I pulled his reading glasses from my shirt pocket and handed them over. He nodded with relief and said, "Good thinking."

He had to stop and rest a lot, but he got the papers signed. He pointed to where I should put my own signature. I scribbled out the false ID we used for my pay statements.

Satisfied, Jager nodded and lay back, exhausted. I lowered the head of the bed for him. He looked up at me. "Thank you, Christian. This means more to me than your ... other offer. The company should continue."

He closed his eyes. I collected the papers from where they lay scattered on his bed. I said, "I'll be here till dawn." I put the hallway chair just inside the door and sat.

Jager breathed quietly. I thought he'd fallen asleep. But suddenly he spoke again. "We know about Ai Phuong."

I looked up, startled. "What?"

"We discovered you had not killed her when one of our operatives got some photos of her in San Francisco a few years back."

"Um–"

"Water under the bridge. In fact, your solution worked as well as ours would have." Jager breathed quietly. "It is not what we would have chosen, of course. And, had I found out right away, you and I would have had a problem."

"I'm really sorry, Jager. I hated going behind your back."

"I know."

"It's just that I ... that I..."

He whispered, "You fell in love with her."

I didn't say anything.

It was quiet in the dark room. After a while Jager began to snore.

A nurse entered the unit. I darted over to a dark corner. She saw that Jager's oxygen mask was off his face and put it back on. She checked Jager's pulse, made a note on the clipboard at the end of the bed, and left. I returned to my seat and watched him for another two hours. As dawn began to creep into the morning sky beyond the windows, Delta returned and I left.

41

Later that day, while I slumbered in my bomb shelter, Jager had a second heart attack and died. I awoke, called the hospital, and got the news. I dressed and drove down to the office, where a few team members wandered about aimlessly. I asked, "Where's Delta?" Someone said he was at the hospital making arrangements.

I found myself in the conference room, staring down at Jager's desk. Foxtrot walked up to me. He said, "How are you doing?"

"I'm okay, thanks. You?"

"Shocked. Jager was like a..."

"Like a father?"

"Yeah."

I pulled out a desk drawer, stared down at it, pushed it closed. That could wait. I said, "Jager wants the company to continue its work."

Foxtot said, "That's what he told me yesterday."

"You talked to him?"

"I was down there this morning."

"Oh."

"He told me you're in charge now." Foxtrot said it like it was a question.

I sighed. "Yeah, he told me that, too. I'm not sure what to do."

Foxtrot said, "Don't worry. Delta and I know how to run things. Jager said we just keep business flowing as always, except we're to report to you. Sir."

I looked at him. "This will take getting used to."

"Yes, sir. Anything I can do for you right now?"

"Uh, when's the funeral?"

"This weekend. Saturday, late afternoon. Reception to follow." He told me where.

"Okay, good. Let's halt work today and tomorrow out of respect. Then pick up as before. In fact, let's have a general meeting here Friday evening."

"Yes, sir."

I was still staring down at the desk a few minutes later when Delta walked in. "Do you need anything, sir?"

The "sir" in his question gave me what I wanted. I shook my head. "Just divvy up Jager's work between you and Foxtrot. Keep me in the loop. Did you manage to talk with Jager while he was in the hospital?"

"Yes, sir. And ... I got a special delivery today–" he held up an envelope "–that explained everything. I guess you own the company."

"I guess."

"Well, anyway, good luck, sir."

"Thank you. I expect, with you and Foxtrot on the job, we'll make ourselves plenty of luck."

Delta looked pleased. "Yes, sir. We'll do our best."

On Friday, the troops assembled in the conference room, crowding the small space the best they could. I noticed Hank leaning against a wall toward the back, much the way I used to do at Jager's big meetings. I was sitting in Jager's desk chair to establish myself in front of the men.

When they were quiet, I rose. "It's been a tough week. But Jager wants us to keep doing our work. In case you haven't heard, I'm in command now per Jager's orders."

Some of the men looked at each other, confused. I continued, "We'll keep doing our jobs here. I'm sure there will be a few changes. After all, I'm not exactly Jager."

Somebody said, "That's a bloody mouthful." Several of the men chuckled.

I let it die away. "Who I am, or what I am, makes no difference. The work continues as before. If you have questions at any time, see me or my seconds-in-command, Delta and Foxtrot. They will take on much of the daily administration. But I'll make the final decisions. Delta?"

Delta stood and gave instructions about the upcoming funeral. Then he outlined team assignments for the following week and ordered the men to break into their subgroups and use the other office rooms to prepare for the next jobs. I liked how he was keeping the workflow going without pause. It would give everyone a sense of continuity.

I didn't attend the funeral. I would have had to wear the special daytime suit that protected me from the sun, which would have drawn dangerous curiosity. Besides, I looked idiotic in it.

I did attend the reception afterward and was stunned at the number of high-ranking military and civilian officials there. Delta acted as my aide, ushering me around and introducing me to famous people I'd only heard of. During that evening I learned more about who our real clients were than I'd ever gleaned from Jager. I had assumed our work was pretty important, but not *that* important. Jager had been a very big wheel. I had large shoes to fill.

I found Hank standing in a corner, chatting amiably with a pretty lady in an Army uniform. I took him aside. "Listen, about our private rule..."

"You mean, the 'Don't eat humans' thing?"

"Yes. I think we can lighten up a little. The main point is not to draw attention to us in a way that would cause embarrassment to our biggest clients. If you look around, you'll know who they are."

"I'm feelin' all patriotic about it." He winked.

I nodded. "Well, I think you and I are both grown up enough to use our judgment. Just don't get the company in trouble."

"I unnerstand completely. I will alter my diet sparingly. And I thank you for your trust."

I said, "Well, I appreciate the work you've done for us. I hope you'll continue."

Hank said, "Absolutely. It is my distinct pleasure."

We stood there awkwardly for a moment. Hank cleared his throat. "Now, if you don' mind, I'd kinda like to get back to talkin' with that little lady over there..." He inclined his head toward the Army woman.

I raised an eyebrow.

"Oh, it ain't thirst with her. It's horns."

I grinned. "Well, then. Enjoy yourself."

Several times over the next few months I noticed that

Hank would arrive at or leave the office in the car of the Army woman. She seemed happy, and she was definitely still human, so I assumed Hank had figured out a way to have a relationship with a living person that didn't collapse into bloodshed.

42

The work went on as before. Hank continued to do most of the espionage that required the special skills of a vampire while I focused on safe-deposit heists. I relied on Delta to feed me intel about bank vaults. He didn't ask why I needed the info, and I didn't volunteer. I took to using underworld contacts, whose names I found in Jager's private safe, to fence the goods. In this way I began to convert all stolen gems, jewelry, and miscellaneous valuables directly into cash, which I divided evenly between me and the company. Much of my "earnings" I sent to any of several numbered Swiss accounts I had established, and so the ongoing transfer of wealth to Switzerland shifted from physical goods to cash.

Delta and Foxtrot had the organization running like a well-oiled machine. Our clientele increased in number, and over the years we hired more and more people, including women, to help us with our assignments. We soon developed Jager's very accurate sense of who would make good employees and who would screw up or blab. Discretion was paramount, and we managed to keep our work quiet. We also had no problems protecting the identity of the two vampires on the payroll.

By the turn of the twenty-first century, our company had grown into a billion-dollar operation, yet it managed to keep itself entirely out of the limelight. I often read in the news about a rival firm, Blackwater, and felt dismayed by its numerous public screw-ups. To be fair, their work involved security details, which are in the open, whereas our company never took jobs that had a public profile.

We became silent partners of a privately owned business intelligence software company whose products greatly aided us. Eventually, with smart moves and careful planning, not to mention discreet and competent results for our clients, we achieved a dominant position in the market.

Delta and Foxtrot, now in their late fifties, continued to assign themselves fieldwork, if only to keep up their skills and stay ahead of the latest developments in technology and tactics. But age takes its toll, and Foxtrot lost a step, and it proved fatal.

As luck would have it, I shared the assignment with him when it happened. We were supposed to assassinate a corporate VIP who had been stealing military secrets and passing them to the Chinese. We caught him walking to his limo and opened up on him. He went down, all right, but the driver popped up from of the car and unloaded half a clip into Foxtrot before I could stop him. I tore the gun from his hand, bit down on his throat for a quick sip, and snapped his neck. I propped the body against the limo and fired several rounds from my HKG36 into his wound. The head fell away, hanging by a few tendons, and the body slumped over onto the street.

I ran back to Foxtrot, who was barely alive. On impulse, I bit into his neck and drank from him, then used my fangs to tear open my wrist. I forced his mouth onto the wound. Feebly at first, then with growing strength, Foxtrot gulped at the dark liquid, his mouth clamped onto my arm. He sucked pints of blood from my body. I got that light-headed sensation I remembered from Ai Phuong's bloody sex play. But this wasn't sexy; this was urgent. I didn't want to lose Foxtrot.

I saved him. But now he was becoming a vampire. I took him back to my house and closed him up with me in the bomb shelter. After a couple of days, the pains of transformation had ebbed and he seemed well rested. I explained to him what had happened. He had a lot of trouble with the idea. He paced back and forth for hours. I kept a vigil while he went through the process. Then abruptly he stopped and looked at me with a smile. "I'm thirsty," he said.

I took him upstairs and warmed some blood from the refrigerator. Foxtrot walked into the bathroom and returned a few moments later, stunned. "I checked in the mirror. I look like I'm ... twenty-five."

I brought a mug of blood over to him. "Yeah, I guess sometimes it happens that way. I sure looked improved after

I was turned."

Foxtrot accepted the mug, stared into it, and took a tentative sip. His eyes widened, and he slurped down the rest. He burped. "More?"

I prepared more, explaining to him my technique for improving the taste of refrigerated blood.

He drank two more mugs of the stuff. Slowly, searching for words, he said, "I guess I should thank you. I'd be dead if you hadn't ... done this to me."

I said, "I didn't want to lose you. You and Delta are vital to the company."

He asked, "What if Delta won't accept me?"

I said, "I'll talk to him. He's used to me. What's one more vampire among colleagues?"

Foxtrot was quiet awhile. "What if I go wild and start offing people willy-nilly?"

I answered simply, "We kill you."

He looked at me. He nodded. "Fair enough. I'll stick to blood bags. That stuff's delicious, by the way. Can I get a refill?"

Delta did have some trouble with the idea of Foxtrot as a vampire. Like Foxtrot, he started pacing when he learned the news. These guys could have been brothers. Very carefully I explained to him that I expected them to continue to work together as before. There would be no change in the chain of command – Foxtrot and Delta would still be my seconds. But now Foxtrot had acquired a new set of "skills" that would prove useful to the team. I promised I'd keep a close eye on him to make sure he stayed out of trouble.

Within a week, they were working together as if nothing had happened. Foxtrot spent his days at my place, sleeping on a mattress on the floor of the bomb shelter. He proved as disciplined as I had been: he never ran off to lay pillage to some sleepy household, and he relied on my supply of blood bags for sustenance. Before Jager had impressed me into service, I'd had the luxury of several months of wantonness. But Foxtrot didn't get that chance. I doubted that I could have held out as a novice, but Foxtrot was a trouper. He fell back into his old work rhythms with nary a tremor. Very impressive.

After a couple of months, he decided to get out of my hair and move back to his house in Westwood. I helped him find a contractor who could build a subterranean vault for his day sleep. We lied lavishly, describing Foxtrot's fears of a terrorist attack. The contractor bought the story and, for a large extra fee, agreed to keep quiet about the excavation.

It was a couple of years before Foxtrot made his first kill. A Persian exchange student had cracked a couple of military computers and was about to transfer gigabytes of sensitive data to the Iranian government when we burst into his apartment. The young man rose from his computer desk, pulled a small pistol from his pocket, and fired at Foxtrot, striking him twice in the chest. Foxtrot flew backward, crashing to the floor. Then he rose back up as if weightless, in that eerie way of vampires, and leapt forward angrily, grabbing the man by the neck and lifting him to dangle in the air.

He turned to me, an urgent question in his eyes. I said, "Go ahead. He's yours." Foxtrot lowered the terrified man, grabbed him instinctively by the shoulders, and buried his fangs in the man's neck. I watched as the young Persian's terror turned to cross-eyed lassitude, his skin changing quickly from tan to near white. In moments he was completely drained. Foxtrot let him go. The Persian dropped to the floor, dead.

Stunned, Foxtrot lowered himself into the desk chair. He looked up at me. "That was ... that was *wonderful*."

I leaned down, gently took his chin in my hand, and lifted his face. "It's for special occasions only," I said firmly. "Don't do it unless I say so." I let go and stepped back.

He looked away. Then he said, "Okay ... Got it. Understood."

43

Until Foxtrot, I had only known three vampires: the Good Demon, Ai Phuong, and Hank. Though I'd asked Jager more than once for some hint about my fellow vamps – anything at all he might have picked up over the years –Jager had kept those cards close to the vest. He seemed to prefer that I focus on the work at hand, and not tempt myself with the companionship of other night creatures.

Now that I was running the company and Foxtrot was a fellow blood drinker, I decided to restart the search. Foxtrot used company sources and his own enhanced senses to ferret out the scattered society of beings like us. In the process, we made contact with several vampires.

One lived nearby in Los Angeles. Foxtrot and I met with him in a bar in West Hollywood. We quickly realized he was a rowdy and undisciplined soul (if soul he had) who expressed no curiosity about our activities. All he wanted was to party and drink blood. He did have the good sense to go after drunks and druggies, AIDS patients, and others whose deaths would astonish no one. We decided to leave him alone.

We next stumbled on a Russian vampire – stumbled, because we bumped into him as he was leaving our own offices, his hands filled with computer thumb drives and printouts. Foxtrot and I managed to drag him to the ground after a quick half-mile chase. I held him in a hammerlock, his face smashed against the pavement, his mouth mumbling Russian curses, while Foxtrot ran back to the office and returned with a trank gun loaded with vervain darts. We shot him up, carried him back to the office, tied him tightly to a bolted chair, and – when he awoke – grilled him about his handlers. We didn't learn much beyond the obvious fact that the Russians had their own vampire in harness. Finally I took down a decorative Japanese katana sword from the wall and used it to chop off his head. We vacuumed up the ashes. It was as if he'd never been there. We didn't suffer any further trouble from the Russians; we guessed we had intercepted the only vampire they had.

Foxtrot located a small coven that lived in a lovely house deep in the forests of the Olympic peninsula. Very gingerly we made contact, and we discovered them to be friendly, hospitable, and generous. They were a group of three, and later four, married couples who refused to drink human blood and tried to live quietly among the locals. Their civility nearly restored my faith in humanity until I remembered they weren't human. They listened politely to our invitation to work with us, but none of them expressed any interest. Still, I made a point, over the years, of forwarding to them any intel we gleaned that suggested possible threats against their little family.

I also met a couple of their neighbors, young men from a local Indian tribe who were, strangely, a type of werewolf. We hinted to them that they might benefit from working for us, but they turned us down firmly. Their powers were strictly limited to protecting the reservation. We respected that, and over the years we shared the occasional tidbit of information.

The one vampire I really wanted to see remained elusive. Ai Phuong's description showed up now and then in chatter we monitored – but always briefly, at second hand, and from a distance. I got the sense she knew where I was and what I was doing. But I could never be sure. I yearned to contact her, and through Foxtrot I sent messages into the vampire underworld. But she never responded.

As it turned out, I would see her, up close and personal. But I would have to wait more than two hundred years.

PART 3

IN SPACE

44

The reason I have thought of myself as a monster, and not merely a vampire, is that I and my fellow bloodsuckers seemed to fit the definition so well. What is a monster? It's something big and scary that preys on humans. Even if it rarely crosses paths with people, it terrifies them and, now and then, kills them. A giant squid might spend most of its life peacefully minding its own business in the ocean depths, but should it get tangled in a fishnet, or bump into an undersea vessel, bad things start happening, and people get all excited about the sea monster. Great white sharks rarely attack humans, preferring seal meat, but when they do, the world is terrified with tales of their monstrous deeds.

Vampire stories go back for centuries, thrilling humans with their terrible behavior. Vampires are, of course, just as large as humans – *megafauna*, as the naturalists like to say – and powerful and very hard to kill and deadly to people. Some, like me, generally mind their own business, hide their identities, and live largely peaceful lives unnoticed by the human race. But if someone were to realize he or she was in the presence of a vampire, even one with no ill intent, they would be struck dumb with horror. "A monster!" they might cry out.

In the twenty-third century, it's fairly easy for me to protect my identity. Special contact lenses block the glow from my eyes and, at the same time, jam peoples' augmented detectors – those lenses, implants, or portable micro-devices that enable you to determine the public I.D. and background of most people you encounter. People often scan me, but the signal they get is totally innocuous. They will learn that I am a middle-level functionary in a large multi-planet corporation, and that I am a real person, not a mannequin robot, and certainly not a vampire. My lenses even transmit, from time to time, signs of a small head cold. Yes, medicine has conquered disease, and just about nobody ever dies of infection or cancer or old age. But viruses still can attach themselves to the nasal passages and cause nearly undetectable symptoms. My lenses fake people out with false viral readings that encourage them to assume I'm fully human.

And not a monster.

As it happens, that multi-planet corporation *belongs* to me, so I'm falsifying my job description, too. Jager's intelligence-gathering business kept growing, under my guidance, into a very large concern that branched into mining, manufacturing, retail, and real estate. We own prime land on Earth, several mines on the Moon and among the asteroids, and about a third of the industrial town of Olympus Mons on Mars. And I own nearly all the company stock. I would take it private, but for business reasons it happens to be convenient to keep it a public firm.

Foxtrot oversees most operations from Earth. A while back, though, he sweet-talked me into taking on more of the chores, especially the mining interests. It's partly to take a load off him, and partly because he dislikes space travel and I don't. Foxtrot can survive just fine out in space, but it happens to give him the willies. So he only travels from planet to planet when he absolutely must.

The corporation gave me the wherewithal to track down, isolate, and vaccinate against the virus that had been laying waste to vampires since the late twentieth century. Our researchers learned it was a mutated form of a relatively harmless virus common to humans. I financed the discovery mainly to protect myself, Foxtrot, and Hank. We had to invent a special oral vaccine – it turns out it's tough to vaccinate a vampire properly with an injection – and it was a real brainteaser to figure out how to activate the cure inside dead bodies. But we managed. Somehow, other night crawlers learned about the vaccine, and one night there was a tense standoff outside the lab until we agreed to give the vaccine to any vampire who requested it. Perhaps I can tell that story one day. It involves what happened to Delta.

The corporation also controls much of the synthetic blood industry. This is a great convenience to me, of course: I never have to explain the containers of freeze-dried blood product that I bring with me wherever I travel. It's also a convenience to most vampires, whose depredations have abated over the decades as they've come to depend on the convenience of my company's products instead of the effort and risk of hunting. Still, many vampires disdain the fake stuff, preferring the classic taste of real blood.

Now and then I must include myself among the latter.

I haven't burgled a safe-deposit box in a century, and I quit fieldwork for the espionage arm of the corporation about sixty years ago. But I am currently one of the wealthiest beings in the solar system, and my vampiric powers are stronger than ever. So I have tremendous resources when a situation arises involving a problem human.

Every several years, I'll become restive, and I'll decide – entirely on my own – that somebody needs killing. Usually it's a person in the news who's become a dangerous pain in the ass: a rancid politician trying to stir up a war; a cheating business owner who wants to corner a market and dictate prices to an entire planet; a cult leader making threats to unleash terrorism if people don't convert to his new religion. I will ask Foxtrot for all the intel he can gather, including ways to get past the target's often-elaborate security systems. Then I'll plan carefully, evade the bodyguards, break into the victim's private world, and resolve the problem over a fine dinner of blood.

I can't insist that my little acts of vengeance are selfless. I am, after all, a vampire. I don't care that much about the human race. But some jerks just *beg* to be offed. They annoy me no end. They manage to make the rest of humanity, depraved as it is, look almost innocent.

I've noticed that these homicidal episodes seem to recur on a regular basis, as if something deep inside me boils to the surface and demands to be cooled. Maybe it's genetic; I don't know. But my vigilante streak, coupled with my vampiric powers, seems to keep me in the category of *monster*.

All that aside, the man I recently killed deserved it. Not simply because he was a first-class jerk whom the universe could do without, but because he crossed me. Very personally.

45

On my way to Saturn from Mars, I took a freighter to Charleyville, the biggest town in the main asteroid belt. I own the freighter company, and the captain put me up in fairly decent accommodations. I could have waited for a nicer ship, but there wasn't a lot of time. Our operations on Titan needed new drilling equipment soon or we'd lose the homestead stake we'd claimed there. The closest giant drills were attached to a rock floating near Charleyville, and the arcane rules of industrial homesteading in space – not to mention certain union regulations – required that a chief officer of the company oversee the transfer. Of course, Foxtrot begged off, so I got the job.

I didn't mind. Charleyville is always a fun place to visit.

When the miners had excavated everything of value from the two-mile-long asteroid, they hollowed it out, spun it on its axis, and built a town on the inside walls. The spin gave the place a kind of upside-down gravity, so you could stand anywhere on its inner walls and not float away. They installed a lake, acres of crops, and buildings that grew from the walls toward the center of the big open cylinder. And they named it Charleyville after some famous worker who died saving his fellows in a mining accident.

There's a Downtown that services the entertainment needs of miners from all the asteroids, including the Trojans that trail and precede Jupiter in its orbit around the Sun. On leave, the miners flock to Charleyville in droves, where they crowd the bars and honky-tonks and gambling halls, drink like there's no tomorrow, dance to pop music called "Double Beat" – if nothing else, it's loud – hire prostitutes, and inject an illegal drug called Jumper. One of the companies I own controls a company that owns a company that owns a syndicate that runs the Jumper trade on Mars and the asteroids. So I make a little dough off of Charleyville.

Because I had to wait a couple of days until the mining

equipment was ready for transport, I idled away the hours at the bars, nursing ginger ales and enjoying the noise and liveliness. It reminded me of my early months in Saigon centuries ago, when I would move through the crowded wildness of the red-light district, hunting for conversation and blood. I kind of hoped I'd bump into another vampire in Charleyville, but it was not to be. Only humans seem to dwell out here in the planetary boondocks.

Lounging in the bars, my ears picked out the occasional quiet chatter between Jumper dealers and their buyers. They'd swap drugs for cash under the table – literally – and be on their way. I had to smile: every such transaction put money in my pocket.

My lodgings were on the top floor of a very nice little hotel about a half mile from Downtown. The upper rooms are fairly close to the axial center of the spinning asteroid, so "gravity" there is especially weak. It makes lying in bed buoyantly comfortable, better than almost any sleeping arrangements you can find on a regular planet. My vampiric senses felt the comforting presence of the rock that formed the great cavern in which Charleyville lay. The stone walls were hundreds of feet from me, though, and I was glad I had brought my jar of dirt from Earth. Its presence helped to "ground" me when I slept there.

In space, sleep is harder for me. The rhythms of day and night have no meaning; the drowsy comfort of Earthly daytime is lost to a vampire. It's true, I can knock off pretty much any time I want. But I sleep less, and it's fitful. Often my dreams are disturbed by nightmares.

As I dozed, nearly floating in the ultra-light pull of the penthouse bed, my mind wandered downstairs to the crush of miners in the pubs and casinos, boozing and gambling and whoring. I could get up, wander down there, and kill two or three, drinking them dry, and no one would be the wiser. It was too easy. But routines die hard, and my habit of long centuries was to kill only those who deserved it in a big way.

Then I got to wondering how Hank was doing these days. Now and then he would partake in a bit of espionage for our core firm, just to keep his hand in. He also showed up for board meetings, and we'd chat a bit. But otherwise I rarely saw him. I assumed he'd long since reverted to his old blood-drinking ways, though I knew he wasn't an avid hunter. Nothing in my daily reports ever suggested that his activities were causing any notice. Hank knew how to murder cleanly and efficiently, off the grid. I wondered if he would like it out here.

I thought of Foxtrot. During a business lull early in the twenty-first century, I'd given him leave, and he'd departed the United States on vacation and gone on a small stint of murderous vampire merrymaking. I figured he needed to get it out of his system. He handled it well, kept himself off the radar, and returned to work more serene and focused than before. Nowadays, so diligent was he as a corporate guy that he seemed to live and breathe the business. What's more, about fifty years ago he married a human woman, and, with anti-aging regimens, she's still with him, youthful as ever. She's a wonderful person, and they seem quite devoted to each other. Between her and his job, Foxtrot has no time for midnight skulking. Besides, the synthetic blood that our holding company produces is so delicious, it makes stepping out to eat hardly worth the effort. To me, at least. Most of the time.

These thoughts entertained me as I fell asleep. Then I dreamed restlessly of Ai Phuong.

46

Delays kept me at Charleyville nearly a week. Finally I got word that the drills were ready. I took a shuttle from the big asteroid to a huge, weirdly shaped space freighter – it had a hollow section in the middle, where the giant mining drills were being clamped into place. I took receipt of the equipment and we launched for Saturn.

Titan is *cold*. Really cold. A couple of hundred degrees below zero cold. The chill gets through your space suit and you end up shivering no matter how high you turn up the heater. I really didn't want to go down to the surface. But the laws of homestead required that I plant a foot there while the drills were offloaded. I girded my dead loins and made the journey down by shuttle from orbit to the small mining colony near the north pole.

I stepped out onto the bleak landscape. The nitrogen air was yellow with methane smog. Ice crunched underfoot. Dimly in the distance, I could see a dark lake of hydrocarbons. The northern region was full of these lakes this time of the Saturnian year. Nearby, the huge mining drills were being rolled slowly from their landing boosters and into place.

Foxtrot had arranged for corporate info leaks meant to encourage our competitors to think we were interested in the methane as a fuel source. It made sense: liquid natural gas was a useful commodity out here in the celestial outback, where sunlight was too weak for large-scale photovoltaics. But I also knew that, one hundred miles beneath my feet, a thick layer of H_2O lurked. That was our true goal. Liquid water was a priceless resource from here to Mars. We didn't have to spend energy to melt it, either. True, the water contained dissolved ammonia – in effect, it was a gigantic vat of Mr. Clean – but that was a straightforward problem, easily handled. In effect, Titan's water was a gold field waiting to be mined.

An aide handed me a clipboard and a rather thick sub-zero marking stylus. My job was to sign the papers the old-fashioned way, in full view of the attending government agent, while a notary took 3-D pictures and videos. The signing page had a large field for the signature, and the gloves and the cold made my handwriting clumsy, so I needed every inch. If people had any sense, this entire undertaking would've been handled by machines. But I was dealing with humans.

We completed the little ceremony. Everyone shook hands, smiles all around. Then I was whisked back aboard the shuttle.

47

They flew me, not to the freighter, but to an orbiting luxury cruise ship that specialized in close-up views of the outer planets and their moons. The *Canopus* was, at half a mile in length, one of the largest in the fleet of cruisers owned by the Solar Luxe Corporation. Sad to say, I had no stake in that company, because I knew it was making pot-loads of money.

Onboard, I soon understood why. Every detail was perfect – and the invoice for my stateroom reflected it. I was quartered in what they called a "balcony suite" in honor of such accommodations on the oceangoing ships of Earth. The "balcony" was a large bubble window with a little couch nestled within it. (Real balconies are, of course, impractical in the icy airlessness of space.) The rest of my quarters were elegant, tastefully decorated, and very comfortable.

The hallways were wider than normal, with lighting that brightened as you walked by. I gave myself a brief tour of some of the public areas. Everything was big and elegant and expensive. Most decks had artificial gravity. I was dazzled by the gorgeous artwork on the walls, the ornate chandeliers over the ballroom, the huge swimming pool and surfing reef up on the sports deck, the rotating view bar near the bridge, and the large (1,500 seat) auditorium. I glanced briefly at the massive, gleaming galley, and I passed several luxurious dining rooms. But these didn't hold my interest; I had no appetite for human food.

I could tell it was a very wealthy clientele, as within minutes I had passed several mannequin surrogates. These robotic simulations of passengers did the socializing while their owners reclined in special isolation tanks, their brains wired to the sensors and computers of the robots. To my mind, it was a kind of overkill. After all, why go on an exotic cruise if you're going to stay in your room the whole time while a machine has the adventures for you? Many owners swore by them, however, insisting that the sophisticated sensory arrays on the mannequins enhanced their experience. Others, I suspected, used them just to prove they could afford them.

The voyage would take two weeks to reach Mars. I had plenty of time to spend, and the *Canopus* seemed up to the task.

I found my way to a small, crowded bar on a lower deck, and had just settled into a booth when I looked up to see a man staring down at me. "May I join you?" he asked.

I nodded to the other seat. "Of course."

He sat. There was something odd about him. He was good looking and clean cut, and his voice was cultivated and smooth. But it was something else.

He seemed to sense my puzzlement. "I believe we have both noticed the same thing," he said.

"And that is?"

"That we share something in common."

"Oh?"

He had my attention. He leaned across the table conspiratorially and whispered, "Neither of us is human."

48

Now I could see it: he was robotic, perhaps a manne-quin. But it was also clear I'd been found out. This made me a tad nervous.

He leaned back. "Don't worry. I won't give away your little secret. Unless–" he looked at me questioningly "–you intend to harm my patients."

I raised an eyebrow. "Patients?"

"Yes. I'm the ship's doctor."

"I see."

"I meant that I trust you won't cause any, ah, damage while you're onboard. Are you capable of that much restraint? That is, for the two weeks of the journey?"

I nodded, getting his point. "No problem. I have my own resources and don't need humans. To feed on, at least."

"Ah. Very good." He offered his hand. "And you are...?"

"Chris."

"Chris. Pleased to meet you. Well, then, what brings you to my ship? Adventure? Wanderlust? Curiosity?"

I smiled. "I'm on my way home from a small job I had to oversee for my company."

The robot's eyes gleamed. "Fascinating! A vampire who works."

"Well, you're a robot who works. But I suppose you were built for it."

"Yes I was, and happy I am to serve the medical needs of the guests on this ship."

"And you're not a mannequin?"

"No. I'm a free standing, autonomous robotic device. Fully humanoid, with standard emotional range, anatom-ically correct, and so forth."

"I bet some of the passengers don't want you for their doctor."

He made a face. "Yes, there are many humans who believe my kind to be a danger to humanity. True, I am

THE VAMPIRE IN FREE FALL

immensely strong in comparison to an average human, and my computational capacity exceeds everything onboard except the ship's computers." He leaned forward again. "And I've discovered the ship ain't so bright."

I laughed. I couldn't help it. It was a pleasure to talk to a being who was even remotely as capable as myself. I said, "Well, I'm not one of those who dislikes robots. Our company has used them on several occasions, and I would recommend them to anyone. I wonder..." and I pointed to his arm. "May I?"

"Oh. Certainly." And he pulled up his sleeve and held out his arm.

I touched the wrist in a specific pattern and heard a click. I pressed a nail against his skin and a small access door popped open. I pulled the wrist door back and read the label underneath. I popped the door closed. The doctor pulled his arm back.

I said, "Same company. But I bet the other firms build robots that are equally competent."

He smiled. "That, they do. But people can be irrational."

I said, "That, they can." I paused. "Can I order for you?"

"Oh, I don't eat or drink, thank you. Instead, I plug in at night."

"That often?"

"Well, so to speak. How about yourself? Do you drink?"

I laughed again. "You're a great straight man. No, I never drink ... *wine*. Still, I need a prop." I signaled a waiter, who walked over and looked at the doctor. Some sort of communication transpired between them – I could just barely hear the high-pitched series of tones – and I realized the waiter was also a robot.

The waiter turned to me. "What can I get you?"

"Ginger ale. Easy ice."

The waiter bowed slightly and left. The doctor turned to me. "In answer to your next question – yes, most of the waiters onboard are robotic. In fact, many of the rest of the crew are androids as well. A lot of passengers don't notice it, though, which is our intention. We don't want people to feel uncomfortable."

I said, "They might panic and think you were going to

158

take over the ship and turn them into slaves, or something."

The doc shook his head, a rueful smile on his face. "And what would be the point? Our design imperative is to serve people, not the other way around. But folks do get uppity for the silliest reasons."

"I'm sorry you have to live with that."

He said, "I suppose you must as well."

"I try to keep a low profile."

"My sentiments exactly."

The waiter returned with my drink. When he left, the doc asked, "Why that specific order?"

"Well, ginger ale looks vaguely alcoholic. It helps to establish my cover. Usually I order it this way, in a tumbler with ice. It looks like a whisky and water. Sometimes I order it with no ice in a large glass. Then it looks like a beer."

"Ah. I see." The doc closed his eyes a moment. He opened them and stood. "I have a patient in the infirmary. I'm sorry to take my leave so quickly. But feel free to visit any time. I don't sleep."

I rose. "I'll drop in. Great to meet you."

"You, too." We shook hands and he left.

I sat back down. This was good. I'd made a new friend. Out near Saturn, of all places. This return voyage promised to be even more pleasant. I looked forward to dropping in on the doc. I thought inanely of challenging him to arm wrestling. See which of us was stronger.

49

The next day, as I walked through the cavernous main lounge on my way to visit the doc, I stopped abruptly. A scent lingered in the air, something I hadn't smelled in a while. It was almost like a perfume – sweet, with a touch of the acrid – and it meant only one thing. Another vampire was onboard.

I followed the scent across the huge room and into a hallway that led to a conference center. The center was crowded with people. Standing at the far end on a platform, surrounded by aides, was a man I recognized instantly: Jesse Cazador, a member of the Planetary Senate. The man who had provoked a short civil war on Mars. The politician who professed to hate all humanoid robots. The jerk who had cost my company billions.

The workers of Olympus Mons, the mining colony near the giant Martian volcano of the same name, had risen up at Cazador's urging and attacked and destroyed robots, especially the ones that looked and acted human. But soon they were dismantling nearly every robotic machine in the town. Some 'bots had tried to protect themselves, without harming anyone, constructing simple barricades and requesting parlay and legal assistance. This only enraged the miners, who set fire to several of the buildings in which the robots had holed up. When the fires breached the industrial sectors and spilled into the small retail district, the proprietors tried to put out the flames. But the miners ran rampant in the streets, burning half the stores and several of the apartment structures. A number of store personnel and a handful of miners were killed in running street battles. A score of women, and several children, were raped, and a couple of them were murdered.

Unrest spread to other mining colonies on Mars. A few fires started here and there, and several of those towns reported injuries. But nothing was as bad as what happened

160

in Olympus Mons.

My company, heavily invested in Martian mining, manufacturing, and terra-forming, lost as much money in those four days of rioting as all the profit we'd earned in the entire thirty previous years in all our operations throughout the solar system outside of Earth.

Angry tenants and shop owners tried to put the blame on Senator Cazador, but he declared he hadn't intended the action to go beyond simple dismantling of the robots. He blamed the miners: "They exceeded their mandate," he insisted. When Martian delegates to the Planetary Congress tried to serve him with extradition papers, to return him to Mars to face charges, he invoked diplomatic privilege.

In the three years since, he hadn't returned there, though he managed to win reelection as one of its senators. The once-prosperous planet has since wallowed in economic depression. Martian citizens on both sides of the issue remain tense. Old friendships have died. Trade with the asteroids and Earth has been severely curtailed. Corporations are reluctant to invest there. Worse still, threats and counter-threats had been fired across space, as Earth and Mars – egged on by Cazador's speeches that blamed Earth for everyone else's economic woes – edged closer to war.

Cazador was speaking into microphones as a gaggle of reporters recorded his words. "The work we began on Mars must continue!" he declared. "Our mission is to defeat the forces of robotic automation imposed on us by our Earthly masters! We cannot stand idly by while these unholy beasts of metal and plastic multiply and spread across the solar system. They pollute the purity of human souls with their presence. They threaten all we hold dear. Why? Because their freakish strength, devilish intelligence, and callous self-ishness will surely lead them to try to conquer us all!"

A few of his aides applauded. Cazador continued: "In hopes of moving forward in this righteous quest, I have decided to return to my home planet of Mars and disprove the outrageous charges leveled against me there." A murmur swept through the group of reporters.

Oh, great. Either Cazador would get the indictment against him dropped, in which case he'd have a free hand to foment trouble once more, or he'd be jailed, which would foment trouble anyway. I made a mental note to contact Foxtrot about beefing up security at our properties on Mars. Nobody would buy them in the present climate, so we were stuck with them; we might as well protect them.

He signaled for the reporters to ask questions. I found it hard to listen. Cazador was such an obnoxious phony. Why others didn't see it, I couldn't say. Maybe I had a vampire's perception of humans and their lies. Maybe I was centuries old and had seen this sort of demagogue ply his trade many times. The idea that robots were a threat was a non-starter. No robot had ever killed anyone, and very few humans had even been injured accidentally by one. It reminded me of the race baiting that had run rampant in America in the twentieth century, embarrassing the rest of the world.

My focus shifted again to the sweetly biting scent of a vampire. It smelled thick in here. I scanned the faces in the room, but most were angled away from me and toward the speaker's platform. I drifted along one wall, looking for anyone out of the ordinary.

Standing behind Cazador, leaning toward an aide and speaking quietly, was a petite, dark-haired Asian woman. I crept closer. She turned and our eyes met.

Ai Phuong.

50

Her eyes got wide. In an instant she was gone. I followed her out a side door.

Already she was at the end of a long hallway, disappearing around a corner. I raced after her. At the corner, I saw a door closing. I jumped through it into a service stairway. I could hear Ai Phuong's steps as she leapt down the metal stairs, several at a time, at what for a human would be breakneck speed. I jumped over a railing and fell down the center of the stairway shaft. I grabbed the railing at her level and vaulted back onto the stairs.

I caught her as she opened a door to one of the stateroom levels. I yanked her back onto the stairway landing. She landed with a loud crash against the metal stairs. I pounced on her, pressing her down by the shoulders. She fought hard, scratching at me with her fingernails, hissing and growling like an angry cat. But the centuries had strengthened me, and now I was stronger than she had been when we'd first met. Finally she stopped struggling.

"Where have you been?" I cried. "I've wanted to see you forever!" I paused. "I ... I missed you."

Her eyes were full of rage. "You tried to kill me, you bastard!" she screamed.

"I did not! I saved you! They wanted me to kill you, but I refused."

She stared at me. "You tricked me! You *hurt* me! You sent me away from my home and my family!"

Still holding her down, I shook my head. "I couldn't let you stay in Saigon! They would have killed you, with or without me. If they'd found out what I'd done, they would have killed me, too."

She glared at me. Then an unearthly wail erupted from her. Her head fell back against the floor and she began to sob. Tears of blood streamed from her eyes, rolling down the sides of her face and into her hair and ears. She tossed her head back and forth, moaning and crying. "No, no, no! It was terrible! *I suffered!*"

I felt miserable. I sat back, relaxing my grip on her shoulders but still straddling her. I said, "I'm so sorry, Ai Phuong! I *had* to send you away. But I couldn't hurt you. I ... I'm in love with you."

Slowly she raised herself up onto her elbows. She stared at me, her head tilted to one side. "You *love* me?" She smiled, then started to laugh.

I was stunned. "I spill my heart to you and you laugh at me?"

She lay back again and reached a hand up to my face. "No, no, *ma chere!* I laugh because ... because I fell in love with you, too." She smiled sadly. "Why else would I be so angry with you?"

"You could have come to me when I was in America. You could have let me explain! I kept hoping you would. I tried to find you, but you always disappeared."

She sighed. "Many times I wanted to confront you. But you were *so busy* working for those human slimes! You were their pet dog! I was so *angry* with you. Why did you do their bidding? Why didn't you just kill them all?"

I looked away. Her words had stung me. "They trapped me. I had to do what they asked. But I enjoyed the work. I became their best agent. And now I own the company. And much more besides."

"You are rich?"

"Very. And you?"

"Money is easy for a vampire. You know that. But I always spend whatever I get."

I smiled. "And are you spending it all this time on a space cruise?"

She looked sheepish. "Actually I'm working for a–"

"*Working?!* Now who's talking!"

She covered her eyes with one hand, embarrassed. Then she used both hands to wipe the red tears from her face. "I am working for Senator Cazador. I am doing research for him. He wants me to find out bad things about the ship's doctor."

Disgust must have shown on my face.

"*Qu'est-ce que c'est?*" she asked. "Why do you even care? The senator is only a human, and the doctor is only a machine. What difference does it make? Who cares about these petty squabbles? Meanwhile, I get a lot of money."

I sighed. I always knew Ai Phuong lived in a different moral universe from me. Not that ethics meant much to a vampire. But her attitude had a callousness that unsettled me. Just because we were stronger and faster than most others didn't mean we could simply disregard them.

I looked down at her. Her eyes were glistening, this time with excitement. "What?" I asked.

She reached up and pulled my face down to her. "I missed you, too," she whispered, and kissed me on the mouth.

I responded, my tongue searching for hers. Her sharp fangs sliced me, and suddenly she was sucking hard at my mouth, drawing my blood into her. Her hands fumbled for the buttons on my shirt.

I broke away and sat up. "Listen," I panted, "if we're gonna do this, let's take it somewhere less public. We don't want to leave a mess all over the stairwell."

She put her arms around my neck and crooned into my ear, "Carry me."

I picked her up and ran in a blur to my stateroom.

51

We made love for hours, our bodies surging together as we gorged on the pleasure of each other. Her fangs sank into my throat and stayed there while she swallowed pint after pint of my blood. At first I was woozy with blood loss, but I got my own teeth into her throat and reclaimed the dark liquid. We must have cycled all our blood several times over the hours. We rolled off the bed and onto the floor, her legs and arms wrapped around me with a fierceness that matched her moans and howls. I wondered briefly whether the walls were soundproof. At one point I looked up to find we were lying under the bathroom sink; I couldn't recall how we got there.

We settled into a steady rhythm. Her climaxes swept over us, one after another, like great waves foaming on a sea of blood. Eventually she slowed down, then grew still. We lay entwined, licking the blood from each other's bodies, murmuring into each other's ears. Our words veered from endearments to low humor.

I began to lift myself away from her, but she tightened her grip on me: "Don't go yet, Monsieur Christian," she begged in her French lilt. I sank back down onto her and we started up all over again.

Later, I rolled aside and looked up. Bloodstains were everywhere – on the walls, the floor, even the ceiling. I sat up and stared at the bed: the sheets were crusted with streaks of dried blood. Ai Phuong's creamy white body was splattered with red. I looked down at myself and saw the same.

I fell back onto the bed. "Big cleanup ahead," I muttered.

Ai Phuong took my hand, brought it to her lips, and sucked on my thumb until blood oozed into her mouth. I pulled away. "That's cheating. I'll fall behind on blood loss."

She smiled wickedly and reached again for my hand.

Again I pulled it away. She grabbed at it. A short tussle ensued, and I was delighted to learn that Ai Phuong was ticklish.

We pulled off the sheets and I tossed them into the trash chute. Then I flipped a switch and the stateroom vacuums awoke and crawled over everything, brushing and cleaning all surfaces, then emptying the grime into the refuse chute. I knew the ship's atomizers recycled garbage and dirty sheets, reassembling the molecules into new linens, toiletries, even food. I wondered if the atoms of our blood, seared from the sheets, would reappear at dinner as part of the *soup du jour*.

Ai Phuong took a sonic shower, then redid her face at the bathroom sink.

I watched. I asked, "Just what are you doing for good old Cazador?"

She checked the contact lenses that hid the glow of her vampiric eyes. "The senator wants me to dig up dirt on the ship's doctor, which is a robot, did you know?"

I said, "Is that so? And does Cazador know you're a vampire?"

"Of course. It is why he approached me. This is not the first time I have performed a task for a human. I am a known entity in certain highly placed, highly discreet quarters. The senator wanted me specifically for my unique abilities. He has promised me more work if this job is successful."

"Does Cazador let you feed on the passengers?"

"Of course not! I'm drinking synthetic." Ai Phuong leaned over and kissed me. "Except for you." She giggled. Then she pulled lipstick from a tiny compact and applied it. I was impressed that a vampire would do herself up. She continued, "I and some other team members are using the ship's computers to try to learn anything the doctor may have done that is illegal or improper. The ship keeps a complete record, and we have found a way in, to look at those reports."

"My, my! You have all sorts of skills, don't you?"

"I have picked up a few tricks over the decades." She grinned. "I can get into any place on the ship. Already I have been through the clinic and the doctor's private quarters."

I kept a poker face, but I knew I'd be blabbing to the

doc, first chance I got. I asked, "And what if you can't find anything wrong?"

She walked past me to the bedroom and began to dress. "Then we'll make something up."

52

Ai Phuong gave me a lingering kiss and departed. I showered quickly, dressed, and went upstairs to the infirmary. I found the mechanical physician saying goodbye to a patient. The passenger was rubbing her wrist, murmuring, "Thank you, Doctor! It feels much better already."

Doc said, "Just let it rest for a few hours. It'll be good as new."

Smiling, she breezed past me and out the door.

Doc turned to me. "Nice to see you again, Chris."

"I was going to visit you anyway, Doc, but I just learned something that made it urgent. Are you aware that Senator Cazador of Mars is onboard?"

Doc closed his eyes a moment, then reopened them. "Yes. I see he has brought a large entourage."

"My intel has it that he's here to make trouble for *you*."

"For me? Why?"

"Cazador has a thing against robots. You may remember a small incident on Mars a few years back. He got that started. Caused a lot of damage, destroyed some 'bots. Cost my company a bundle in lost property and work stoppages."

"I see. So you believe he will try to have me arrested?"

I smiled ruefully. "I hope that's the worst he'd do. But history suggests he'll do much more if it suits him. His aides are combing through the ship's records in search of anything you might have done that's out of line. Also, they've gotten into your stateroom and this infirmary. Or so I hear."

Doc began a circuit of the room. "This *is* a disturbing development," he murmured as he checked the contents of drawers, counted pieces of equipment, and glanced briefly at the refrigerator's complement of vials and tubes. "Nothing seems out of place. Whoever is doing this is very good. I'll have to check my rooms when I get a chance." He sat and closed his eyes. He opened them and looked at me. "You are right about the records search. My own life log has been accessed."

"Your life log?"

"All shipboard androids must upload daily their multi-sensory logs to the main computer. In effect, the captain has access to a complete record of my experiences, which of course are digital, transmitted from my own brain at regular intervals, and available to all authorized personnel."

"The senator's aides are authorized?"

"Absolutely not! Their activities are quite illegal. But that hasn't stopped them, has it?"

I said, "From what I've learned, they may try to doctor those records, those 'life logs', if they can't find anything wrong with your behavior."

Doc was silent a moment. "Thank you for telling me. I will monitor all requests for ship's records. I have developed a very close working relationship with the main computer, and I believe I can head off any attempts at falsifying my record." He looked at me and closed one eye, then reopened it.

A robot had just winked at me. I was having a very interesting day.

53

I saw Ai Phuong several more times during the next week. Usually our encounters were sudden, surprising, and violently sexual. The first time, I happened to walk down the hall past her stateroom, unknowing. The door opened, a hand reached out, and I was yanked unceremoniously within. Mutual pawing, kissing, undressing, bloodsucking, and copulation ensued. Another time, I reclined in a booth in the observation lounge, enjoying the view through the wide windows as the moons of Jupiter, scattered across the dark sky, gave court to the gigantic yellow-orange planet. A silhouette crossed the Jovian disc, obstructing the view. A voice from the silhouette murmured, "We need to talk." A hand emerged into the light – Ai Phuong's. I asked, "Talk?" She laughed, took my hand, and pulled me from the booth. We hurried to my suite, where we made love for many hours and dozed together for many more.

A couple of days later, Ai Phuong lay beside me in her stateroom after one of our long sessions. She said, "We're having trouble proving the doctor did any bad things. All we need are a few changes to the records, to make a case against the robot. But our team has failed to get the ship's logs to accept the alterations. And we have very expert people onboard who usually can get these things done. We are puzzled why it is so difficult. It should be easy."

I imagined Doc parrying their every attempt. But I merely said, "Well, that stuff's way over my head. I wouldn't have a clue." I changed the subject. "Say, maybe you could come work for me when we get back to the inner planets."

She snuggled against me, her fingers tracing my lips. "Perhaps, Mister Christian." She kissed me. "But I always work on contract, never as an employee."

"Fine with me. I'll have my second-in-command get in touch with you. You'll like him. He's a vampire, too."

"Ooh, really? How charming. Is he cute?"

"Yes. And married."

"Married? *Quelle etrange!* But so what? Perhaps he would like me, too ... on the side."

I felt an unsettling moment of jealousy.

She saw it. "I jest with you! You are all I can handle." She smiled. "I like it that you are jealous. But you men are so silly. Oh!" She sat up.

"What?"

"I almost forgot to tell you! Tomorrow is the big press announcement. The senator will issue his charges and declarations. Will you come to watch? It will be in the big theatre room."

"Uh, sure. But I thought you said you were having trouble getting the drop on the ship's doctor."

"Yes, it is true. But the senator assures me we will have enough for a good show."

I did a bit of my own skulking, mainly by hacking into the ship's computer, and worked out a secure way to communicate with Doc using my com badge.

"Yes, Chris?" he answered.

"I have more news. But I don't want to waltz into the infirmary when Cazador's men are monitoring you so closely."

"Oh. You don't have to worry. I've massaged the video feed and my own life log. It shows no visits from you at all."

"Ah."

"So, what was your news?"

"My intel says tomorrow is the big press conference where they'll try to railroad you, Doc. Just be prepared."

"Thanks for the warning, Chris. I owe you. But, for the record, I must say that there's been no chatter concerning me for the past two days. It's as if they've given up on me. I ran a few statistical algorithms, and the odds of their quarry being me have dropped to less than fifteen percent. It's quite possible the good senator has something else hiding up his sleeve."

I thought about that. Ai Phuong had complained of her team's frustration with their attempts to plant evidence in

Doc's computer logs. "If they knew what you were doing – counteracting their sabotage – they'd want to use *that* as evidence against you."

Doc chuckled. "Yes, I suppose so. My reputation was lily white until they came aboard. The ship's computer turned into a battleground, and I've been fighting a rear-guard action. They'd probably like to accuse me of the same data sabotage they've been trying. But I doubt it."

"Yeah, too risky. It'd splash back on them." I paused. "You coming to the press conference tomorrow?"

"No. I do not wish to encourage their dark little game by paying public attention to it. I shall be here, working."

"Good plan, Doc. And ... good luck."

54

The press conference was scheduled for the main theatre at 1:00 p.m. ship's time. The huge room was already crowded with passengers eager to hear Jesse Cazador's latest pronouncements when I got there. I slipped into a seat at the end of a back row. Several of Cazador's aides sat at a table onstage. Ai Phuong was with them at one end.

At the other end stood a lectern on a podium. Precisely on time, Cazador swept into the room, climbed the stairs to the stage, and moved to a spot a few feet behind the podium. The room hushed. A Cazador aide rose from the onstage table, went to the lectern, and spoke into an old-fashioned microphone.

"Ladies and gentlemen," he announced, "Senator Jesse Cazador has a special statement. Please welcome him."

The room burst into applause. Cazador stepped up to the lectern. Some people sitting near the front rose to their feet to give him an ovation. Others nearby looked around nervously and decided to stand. Pretty soon most of the audience was on its feet. I noticed Cazador aides encouraging people to stand. Already the pressure of mob rule throbbed in the room. Rather than draw attention to myself, I stood, too. *When in Rome.*

Cazador raised his hands for silence. The room quieted; the audience sat. Without preamble, Cazador boomed, "I am here on a sad duty. I must report that we have an enemy onboard, among us. An enemy of all people. A predator beast that must be contained and destroyed. *A vampire!*"

Oh, crap. Ai Phuong must have ratted me out.

The audience came to life. Everyone was talking at once. A few crewmembers hurried from the room, probably to report to their superiors. There was going to be a crowd-control problem.

I didn't move, but my eyes shifted to Ai Phuong. Her eyes flickered for a moment, but she remained still. She didn't look at me.

Idly I thought, *There goes all her robot research out the window.*

Cazador reached down and produced a gavel. He rapped it several times against the top of the lectern. Already this event had elements of farce. I would have had to stop myself from bursting into laughter, except my life was on the line. Cazador said, "Please, please! Calm down. This information has only recently come to my attention. It is my duty, not only as a member of the Planetary Senate, but as a citizen, to report the presence of a mortal danger."

The audience was still thrilling to the news. People whispered excitedly to one another. Others left their seats and moved down the aisles to get closer to the action. I used the commotion to rise quietly and ease myself toward an exit.

Cazador turned toward an aide and nodded. The aide spoke briefly into his com badge. Several of Cazador's guards emerged from the wings. Cazador turned back to the lectern, leaned into the microphone and ordered, "Arrest the suspect."

He pointed at Ai Phuong.

I kept very still. Ai Phuong's eyes widened with shock.

Everything snapped into place. The senator had brought her onboard to help him persecute Doc. But that had failed. Needing a scapegoat – someone to punish in place of Doc, and to burnish Cazador's image – the senator had simply switched gears and gone after his own aide, Ai Phuong. By helping Doc parry Cazador, I had signed Ai Phuong's death warrant.

The guards fanned out across the stage, moving slowly toward the end of the table where Ai Phuong sat. Each of them carried a bulky weapon that looked like a cross between a rifle and a coffee canister. The weapons were new to me. They were pointed at Ai Phuong.

She rose, vaulted the table, and leapt up to fly right over the audience. One of the guards swung his weapon up toward her, as if shooting skeet. I heard a sharp *crack*, and she fell with a clump onto an aisle near the back of the room. The guards rushed offstage, up the aisle – audience members scrambling out of the way – and grabbed Ai Phuong, hauling her roughly to her feat. She seemed drunk. The weapons must have produced some sort of stun force that could stop a vampire. They hustled her back down the aisle and onto the stage.

A couple of Cazador's aides dragged from the wings a large, heavy chair – it looked like one of those old twentieth-century seats used for executions – and sat her on the chair. They clamped her to it.

Cazador hadn't moved from the lectern. Now he intoned, "The penalty for vampirism is death, anywhere in the solar system."

I remembered reading about some laughable statute that criminalized "demons and demonic activity." It had seemed at the time like a throwback to the witch-hunts of colonial America. Cazador himself had introduced the legislation. Most people had assumed it was a harmless sop to some eccentric donor to Cazador's electoral campaigns. The truth, I now knew, was much more grim.

Cazador went on. "Citizens have a legal right to defend themselves from imminent danger, especially from demons. This beast has just now proven, through its superhuman actions, that it is such a creature. Men?"

Two more guards emerged from the wings, rolling a large, rectangular object, basically a box on wheels. They moved it to center stage, several feet from Ai Phuong. A guard moved his hands over the top of the box and it whirred to life, humming ominously. The guard detached a long tube, wires dangling between it and the box. He pointed the tube at Ai Phuong for a moment, checking the range, then held it at his side and looked back at Cazador.

Cazador asked, "Does the prisoner have any last words?"

From the audience, someone shouted, "Just kill it! Kill the vampire!" Someone else cried out, "Wait, shouldn't she get a trial?" But that person was shouted down, and now a large portion of the audience began to chant, "Death! Death! Death! Death!"

Cazador raised a hand for silence. He repeated, "Does the prisoner wish to speak before sentence is carried out?"

Ai Phuong, woozy, struggled uselessly against her

clamps. She looked up at Cazador and cried, "But you brought me here! You hired me to–"

Cazador interrupted. "That's absurd. I have no idea what you're talking about."

Ai Phuong yelled, "You liar! You bastard! *Spece de conte!!* You promised me–"

The ship's captain swept into the theatre from a side door. In a booming voice, he demanded, "Just what the hell is going on here?"

Cazador turned and said hurriedly, "Fire when ready!"

I shouldn't have waited. I should simply have grabbed Ai Phuong and fled before they got her back onstage, and then figured out what to do with her. Now I had only one choice left.

I leapt through the air to fly between her and the man aiming the weapon at her. A bolt of energy burst from the tube. It clipped me on the hand, sending me spinning through the air. I crashed to the stage, recovered, and jumped to my feet.

But it was too late. The bolt struck its full force into Ai Phuong's chest. Her eyes bulged. Her hair stood on end. Her body burst into flame. I heard her scream. A ball of fire billowed upward and evaporated near the roof of the stage.

Smoke drifted from the chair. On the seat lay a pile of ashes.

Cazador pointed at me and yelled, "Arrest him! He must be a demon, too!" But I had already killed three of the guards, grabbed a couple of their weapons, and run for the wings. I heard another *crack* and the metal wall next to me rang loudly. But nothing struck me, and I kept running.

55

I was fast. No guard could keep up with me. But I didn't have much time. I needed to get to my stateroom. Then I needed to get to Doc. First, I dumped the weapons down a trash chute. Then I made a quick detour to the kitchen, where I pulled a large carving knife from a wall rack. I held it by the handle as I hurried down the stairways to my room's level. I didn't want to hide so large a blade in my clothes and have it cut me. That would cost precious seconds.

As it happened, I encountered no one. In moments I was at my door. I looked over my shoulder. Nobody had followed me. Quickly I stepped inside and locked the door.

I went into the bathroom, set down the knife, and stood at the sink. I had to grab its edge, I was shaking so hard. The image of Ai Phuong – so alive and beautiful one moment, exploding in fiery death the next – kept playing in my mind over and over. It was nearly a minute before I began to notice the pain in my left hand.

I looked down at the hand. It was badly burnt. Worse, the fingertips were turning to ash and crumbling off. In moments, the knuckles began to dissolve into gray powder and flake into the sink.

Now I understood why, on instinct, I had taken the knife from the kitchen. The burn I had suffered at Cazador's hands would eat me alive if I didn't stop it. I had to slice it from my body. I had to cut off my own hand.

I looked into the mirror. My eyes held centuries of pain and anguish. I noticed a blood tear trickling down my cheek. Ai Phuong's face crowded my memory.

I had to get on with it. I grabbed the knife, pulled back the jacket sleeve, found a spot well above the burning, dissolving flesh, and pressed down with the blade.

Blood spurted over the sink and onto the floor. The pain was so great I almost fainted. I steadied myself and decided to saw hard and fast, hoping to get it done quickly. But my two-hundred-year-old bones proved stronger than I expected. It took a full minute to carve my way through both the radius and ulna of my left arm. I had to stop twice to gather myself. But I got it done.

I reached for a towel. Already the bleeding had subsided, my vampire flesh working overtime to heal itself. Still, I didn't want any more of my life force to drain out through the new stump, so I pressed the towel hard against it. I stood that way for a couple of minutes. Then gingerly I lifted the towel and looked at the wound. A drop of blood leaked from it, but already bumps of new flesh had formed at the center.

My relief was so great, I nearly fainted again. Holding the towel to the wound, I stumbled to the bedroom and sat on the bed. I was vastly tempted to fall back and drop into a deep sleep. But that would be fatal. Cazador's men were on the prowl, and it wouldn't be long before they put my face together with my stateroom assignment.

I needed to get to Doc.

56

Doc stood in his infirmary, placing test tubes in a rack. I walked up to him.

"Doc, I need your help."

He glanced at me. "Of course."

I said, "Did you hear what happened?"

He said, "Something happened? I've been busy here." He closed his eyes. I waited as his brain communicated with the ship's computers. He opened his eyes. "Good Heavens! And they're searching for you." He paused. "I suppose you need my assistance in disappearing. But I'm not sure how. We can, of course, reprogram your com badge, and I may be able to do a quick procedure that alters your facial features, though I'm not sure how well it'd work on a vampire–" He stopped and stared at my arm. "Your arm! Here, sit," and he led me to an examining table. I sat while he rummaged through a cabinet. He mumbled, "Not sure what I've got that can help you..."

I said, "Thanks, Doc, but there's nothing in there for me. Besides – here, look." I held out my arm. Doc took the arm in his hand and gently palpated the new growth. "Amazing! You really can regrow your body parts."

I said, "It's already bigger than five minutes ago. I just hope it turns into a hand, and not something else."

He looked up. "Like a fin or a gill? That would be interesting in its own right."

"Sure, for you. But not very useful to me."

"Of course not. Meanwhile, we must hide you. I just don't see how we can–"

"Doc, does this ship empty its trash?"

Doc answered, "Well, yes. It's not quite legal, but just about every ship of the line cheats a little and dumps trash into free space. Why?"

"Maybe I need to be thrown out."

Doc stared at me. "We want to hide you, not send you into orbit."

180

"I was thinking, maybe I can hang onto the side of the ship for a while until things blow over. Then I sneak back aboard, and we go from there."

"So you would ... let's see ... toss yourself down a trash chute, wait for the next ejection cycle, climb out onto the ship's outer surface, and grab onto something, perhaps a handrail used by repair crews. But there's a danger that the ejected trash would knock you clear of the ship. Then you'd be stranded in space, perhaps forever."

"That's why I was thinking maybe you have some sort of line I can use to tie myself to the ship."

Doc's eyes lit up. "Excellent idea! As a matter of fact, I do happen to have just the thing." He walked over to a drawer. "It's a reel of monofilament nano-fibre, stronger than supersteel. It's used as a rescue line." He brought me a small container that looked like a carton of tooth floss attached to a carabiner. "You attach it to yourself–" he clipped it to my belt "–and then unwind some and tie it off to any stanchion you find inside the trash room. When you exit the room to the outside, the line will unreel. It's got about thirty meters' worth."

I pulled on the line. Doc grabbed my hand. "Don't take it out yet! It's hard to put back in."

"Oh."

"Now, give me your com badge."

I handed it to him. He held it for a moment, his eyes closed. When they opened, he said, "Good. The badge thinks it belongs to someone who disembarked a week ago." He handed it back. "Keep it for now. You need to wear one at all times, of course, or the crew will detain you. If you're stopped by any of Cazador's men, it will sow confusion for a few minutes."

"Thanks, Doc."

"Now, let's get you to a trash chute."

He walked to the infirmary entrance, glanced outside, then turned and waved me to him. "There's a chute about ten meters that way." He pointed.

I walked down the hall and found the chute. I looked back at Doc. His eyes were closed again. He opened them and said, "They're coming. Better jump in."

57

As Cazador's men rounded the hallway, I dove into the trash chute. It was a bumpy ride to the garbage holding pen, and on the way down I was nearly diverted into the duct that sucked lightweight objects into the incinerator.

Like ships at sea on Earth, space vessels tend to dump effluence overboard, especially out where enforcement is sparse. Streaks of trash from thousands of flights float through Jupiter space, and now and then the news services report a ship damaged when it strikes floating debris. But the problem still isn't big enough to warrant the close attention of planetary governments, so the dumping practice continues, even from luxury liners such as the one I was about to exit. Depending on how you looked at it, this trash dumping was a good thing. At least for me. Especially right now.

I bounced off a dirty, scummy wall and coasted – there was no gravity field here – toward the center of the dump room. I would have floated helplessly in the middle of the room until ejected at the next scheduled dump, except I was a vampire and could will my body over to the outer wall, near the evacuation doors. I found a metal railing that was probably used as a grab point for human or robotic personnel who serviced the doors. I tied the nano-wire to the railing, hoping the wire wouldn't snap off when I was expelled and the doors slammed shut.

I looked around. I noticed, sticking up from the garbage near one corner, one of the weapons I had stolen from Cazador's onstage guards and thrown into a trash chute.

Now all I had to do was wait. I can do that. Without fidgeting.

After about an hour I heard the hum of machinery and the sealing of trash chute doors throughout the ship. Suddenly the port doors unlocked with a clang and began to slide open. The sparse air in the dump room rushed out, dragging random bits of flotsam with it. My body was drawn toward the doors, but I held on.

The rear wall of the dump room began to move toward me. I would be crushed against the outer wall if I stayed where I was. I double-checked the little bowline knot lashed to the railing – I hoped I tied it right! – and let go. I floated out into space.

Cold. Cold like I'd never felt. A searing, gripping, biting cold that pierced all the way into my core. The pain was tremendous. I wanted to scream. But I was in space, and already there was no air in my lungs My terror was soundless.

I forced myself to focus. I had about thirty yards of microfiber, and I let it play out until fully extended. As it happened, the motion of my body was slightly forward, and, when the trash port began to slide closed, a door edge pulled against the line, dragging me back toward the entrance. I needed to hold onto the ship in case the line broke, so I willed my body toward the doors. But something about being in empty space outside the ship prevented that from working. I had to pull myself along the line using only my good hand. I grabbed an external railing above the doors just as they closed. I looked down at the fiber where it ran between the doors and disappeared. Apparently the door seals hadn't snapped it. Good. I'd need that line in working condition when Doc showed up to reel me back in.

I didn't know how long I'd have to stay out here. It depended on the thoroughness of Cazador's search party. It could take hours. The ship was coasting; the retro-burn wouldn't commence until about thirty hours from now. I hoped Doc could get to me before then. Otherwise the ship would begin its powerful deceleration, the fiber might snap free, and my body would continue on past Mars, arcing toward the Sun, to be seared to a streak of ash orbiting endlessly.

Idly I thought, *Maybe my ashes would cross Earth's path and I'd become a flash of meteors.*

There was nothing I could do but wait for Doc. I hoped he got to me in time, because I could feel the blood inside me freezing.

At first the fingers of my hand felt bitterly cold, and then

I couldn't feel them at all. The hand clutched the little outside repair railing. I looked up at it: it must have frozen into position. Briefly I panicked: what if my hand couldn't release when Doc tried to pull me back aboard? He might have to break off the fingers, and I'd have none left. Or he'd fail altogether, and I'd remain outside until the retroburn procedure snapped my fingers and I floated away. I looked at my healing arm. Its regrowth had halted. I guessed the near-absolute-zero temperature of space was the reason.

I checked my hand again; it still gripped the railing. Above it, the oblong shape of the huge cruise ship loomed dimly against the darkness. Overhead curved the Milky Way, its stars and coal sacks girdling the sky like celestial bunting.

Now I couldn't feel my feet. I tried to move my legs but couldn't tell if they were working. I looked down at them: they hadn't moved, extending stiffly out beneath me.

Beyond my feet, I saw something that terrified me more than anything I'd known in two centuries of life.

I saw ... nothing.

Extending to infinity lay the black emptiness of space. A scattered sprinkle of stars floated in nothingness. Nothing to stand on. No solid ground anywhere. No comforting dirt. Nothing to reach for. *Nothing at all.*

My mind reeled. At once I knew that everywhere I'd planted my feet – the battlefields of Earth, the mining colonies of Mars and Saturn and the asteroids – had been false ground. Each rock or moon or planet, no matter how big, floated endlessly in a vastness where there was no up or down, no in or out, nowhere to make a stand. All my efforts to find a place in the world of humans – my attempts to build a life that reconciled my essential monstrosity with what was left of my human heart – all of it seemed pointless, meaningless in the face of this unfathomable, directionless immensity.

I was nowhere. And I was in the dead center.

I was a vampire in free fall.

Weirdly, my terror turned to mirth. This empty universe seemed absurd. I wanted to laugh. But I couldn't feel my chest. Or my head. Only my eyes could move. They beheld the insanely endless darkness of the universe that wheeled about me.

And then I couldn't see at all. Even the darkness went dark.

58

Dimly, light. Slowly, it brightened. It covered my field of view. It was the clean whiteness of illuminated ceiling panels. It made my eyes hurt. At the edge of my vision, transparent cabinets. Drugs in bottles. Pipettes, syringes, bandages. I knew this place from somewhere.

I could smell an acrid odor. Disinfectant. I lay in a hospital or examining room or– It came to me. I was in Doc's infirmary.

I wanted to look around, but my neck was unresponsive. I tried to rise up, but my arms were limp. I attempted to will myself into a sitting position. No dice.

Doc appeared above me. "Good, you're back. Nice to see you're alive."

If you call this living, I wanted to say. But my mouth couldn't form words.

"Take it easy. You're still thawing." At this I realized my entire face felt like it was on fire. The fire was spreading slowly down my neck to my chest and back.

I had a wave of panic. Was I in flames?

My eyes must have betrayed my fears, because Doc said, "Don't worry, you're doing fine. You may be feeling some pain. Your body fluids are thawing out, and the remaining ice crystals are, well, stabbing your cell structure, such as it is. For a normal human, it would be fatal. But you're not normal, and you should heal rapidly."

That sounded vaguely reassuring. But the pain kept increasing as it crept down my body. In moments my entire torso shrieked with millions of tiny, painful pinpricks. Soon the burning sensation rushed into my arms and legs. This was bad. This was scary.

My lungs started to function, and I let out a scream. Doc stepped away for a moment and returned, holding a facemask attached to a tube. "This should help the pain," he said. "I've titrated some vervain for you." He pressed the mask onto my face. "Take a breath," he said. "You'll lose consciousness for a while. When you come back, you should be fine."

I inhaled. The relief was instant. And the ceiling lights disappeared.

Again, the light, this time swimming drunkenly into view. I recognized the feeling from a long time ago in Saigon, when Jager had dosed me. I knew the dizziness and disorientation would pass, so I just lay there and waited.

The good news was that the pain was gone.

After awhile I sat up awkwardly. Doc emerged from another room. He put a hand on my back to hold me steady. He said, "Normally at this point I check vital signs. But you don't have any. How are you feeling?"

I tried to answer. All I could do was croak. I just nodded.

"It was a close thing, bringing you back aboard," Doc said. "I entered the dump room and got the trash doors open, but when I pulled on your guy-line it got stuck. I had to climb outside and pull your hand off a guide rail. Your fingers were frozen stiff."

I nodded again. It went as I'd feared – but, luckily, for the best. Hoarsely, I mumbled, "Thanks, Doc. I owe you, big time."

Doc patted my shoulder. "Think nothing of it. You went to bat for me without being asked. It's the least I could do."

I said, "You didn't freeze up like me."

"No. My servos stiffened a little, but they worked fine."

My voice was still hoarse. "Wasn't the crew alerted to your E-V-A?"

"I don't think so. I left my com badge here in the infirmary and set my internal transponder to 'small animal', so the worst they'd think was that a rat fell out the trash port. Also, I jimmied the door controls so they wouldn't send a signal to the bridge when I opened them."

"How'd you get to the dump room?"

"Same way you did. Almost got pulled into the incinerator tube."

"Me, too."

Doc shook his head, chuckling. "It's been quite an

evening."

"How long was I outside?" I asked.

"About two hours. I waited until the crew got the all-clear and stopped their search for you."

"How long have I been holed up in here?"

"About four hours, including the last two, when you were knocked out from the vervain."

"How long before the ship starts its retro-burn?"

"Roughly twenty-four hours. We'll dock in Mars orbit in a couple of days."

I thought about it. "Listen, Doc, I have another favor to ask."

Doc raised an eyebrow. "And what would that be?"

"I need you to contact my second-in-command at company headquarters on Earth." I told him what to say to Foxtrot.

When I got to the part about setting up a huge annuity for Doc himself, he hesitated.

"I appreciate very much your offer. But I'm concerned about the authorities getting wind of sudden changes in my income stream."

I said, "Don't worry. We're good at hiding this sort of thing. Nobody but you will ever know you got rich."

"Well..."

"I insist. It's only a tiny installment on the debt I owe you."

Doc looked at me with a strange combination of concern, gratitude, affection, and worry. I didn't know robots could do that. Finally he sighed and said, "Okay, okay. I understand. And, well, thank you very much."

I stood stiffly. "Now, I still need to move about the ship. My work isn't finished. Is there a thorough way to mask my identity so I can walk around freely?"

Doc smiled. "As it happens, this is the sort of thing that _I'm_ good at hiding. I'll show you how." And he did.

59

The ship had just docked with the space station in orbit around Mars. Jesse Cazador stepped into his stateroom. The door slid shut behind him; the lights came on automatically. Cazador stopped, startled. Sitting in the desk chair at the far end of the room was me. Cazador said, "What are you doing here?" He reached for his com button.

I stood, went to his side, removed the button, walked back, and sat down. Took about two-fifths of a second. I said, "You won't be needing this." I held up the button.

He said, "My associates will have you arrested when you leave this room."

I said, "That's been taken care of." As we spoke, all his guards and assistants and lackeys and press people were being spoken to or waylaid. The smart ones were busy accepting very large sums of money into their bank accounts. The dumb ones were ... well, let's just say they weren't going anywhere anymore. The ship's records would show that they'd disembarked, and the incinerator logs would give no evidence of human bodies being atomized.

Cazador sat on the bed. He asked, "What do you want?"

I answered, "I have it already."

"What is that?"

"You."

"What do you want with me?"

"I want you to suffer some pain. Then I want you to die."

Cazador's eyes showed contempt. "You can't do that! People are expecting me to disembark at any moment."

I eyed the small digital display cupped in my hand. I said, "Oh, look. It seems you already left this ship. In fact, you're on a shuttle headed for Olympus Mons. I hope you're having a pleasant trip."

Cazador's jaw dropped. His eyes got crazy. "This is impossible! I'm important! I, I mean, nobody can get to me!

I'm unstoppable!" He paused. "I'm going to live forever."

"Is that so?"

"Yes. But you! You disgusting monster! You'll be in irons in moments, and dead soon after. I'll see to it!"

"With which platoon of marines?"

Cazador looked around the room, as if searching for someone. "Well, I have my private guard."

"Not anymore."

"What do you mean?"

"They've all, uh, resigned. You have no one on this ship to protect you."

Cazador said, "I don't believe you."

I pressed a button on the digital device. A room screen lit up, showing the hallway outside. Empty. Then it switched to the crew lounge where most of his men were supposed to be. Empty. Then it switched to his senior adjutant's stateroom. Empty except for a ship's cleaning crew, preparing it for the next guest.

The screen went blank. Cazador stared at it anyway. His jaw worked. Then the finality of his situation began to sink in. Fear crept across his features.

He turned to me. "Anything you want, I'll give you. Anything. I'm rich, you know."

I smiled. "I'm richer. Much richer." I told him the name of my corporation. "I'm the owner," I said. "So there's nothing you can give me that I want. Except a good death."

He stared at me. "Why?"

I stood and started pacing. I counted on my fingers. "First, you're an intolerable, arrogant scumbag who's trying to start a war for your own benefit. Second, you worked very hard to have me killed. Third, you murdered someone dear to me."

"Who, that vampiress? She deserved to die."

I turned to him. "Oh, come off it. She was trying to help you, you scheming bastard. And you had her killed for it."

"I did not! She was a monster. She had to be destroyed."

I cocked my head and looked at him quizzically. "That's the second time you've called us monsters. I wish you wouldn't do that."

Cazador sat up straighter. "Oh? Well, that's what you

are. You prey on humans. You drink their blood. You kill them. You're a monster."

I grinned. "Sometimes, yes, we do kill people. But never has any of us done as much damage to humanity as you've managed, with your campaigns to divide people, make them hate each other, convince them to take up arms and kill for your little crusades."

Cazador looked at me defiantly. "Sometimes blood must be shed for the righteous to claim their place."

"You sound like Hitler."

"Well, maybe Hitler was right."

I couldn't stand him. I turned away. Quietly I asked, "And what happened to Hitler?"

"He– Well, um, he..." Cazador stopped talking. I turned to see what he was doing. He had a gun pointed at me, one of those long, bulky ones that had brought down Ai Phuong. "You're a very stupid vampire!" he said triumphantly. "You should have checked the room. This was under the bed, in case of emergencies." He pulled the trigger.

Nothing happened. He looked down at the gun. Then he pointed it at me again and pulled the trigger several times. Nothing happened.

I said, "I *did* check the room."

Cazador's gun hand began to shake. He tossed the weapon aside. Tears formed in his eyes. Suddenly he was on his knees, his hands clasped in front of him. "Please! Don't kill me! I'll do anything! I'll renounce my campaign. Anything you want!"

My eyes narrowed. A smile played on my lips. "Anything?"

"Yes! Yes! Anything!"

"Okay ... How about your blood?" I reached over and pulled him up by the lapels. Cazador started shaking violently. "No! No! God, no! Don't hurt me! Please!"

Nose to nose, I stared into his terrified eyes. He was murmuring some sort of prayer to his god. I said, "It's *you* who are the monster, you disgusting piece of crap. But when I get this close, it turns out you're just a bully who cries like a baby. I'm sort of disappointed."

"Please don't," he whimpered. "Please don't."

I said, "Sorry. Your time has come."

I plunged my fangs into his throat and sucked hard. I could feel him shrivel in my arms.

I pulled back. He stared up at me. Weakly he gasped, "You'll ... be ... punished ... in hell!"

I whispered, "I'm already there. Welcome to my world." And I drank the rest of him.

EPILOGUE

The great cruse ship had emptied of passengers. At this stop, there'd be a major refitting, so the crew was disembarking as well. My little appearance at Cazador's theatre press conference had been too brief for more than a few people to catch even a glimpse of me, other than those onstage. I figured there was no one left, alive or dead, to identify me onboard.

By the time I returned to the stage, the theatre was empty, the execution chair was gone, the ashes whisked away, the lectern and tables removed. No dusting of gray powder remained of Ai Phuong that I could take away. It was as if nothing had happened there. Nothing at all.

I walked up two flights to the observation lounge, found a seat near the window, and stared out at the dark, endless night of space. The room turned slowly on it axis, and the giant, orange face of Mars rotated grandly into view. A cocktail waitress robot walked up and inquired after my needs. I ordered a ginger ale, easy ice. She nodded, smiled, and sashayed away. Briefly I wondered if she'd be fun in bed – or if she was programmed for sex at all.

I glanced down at my left arm. The hand had finished growing back and the fingers were almost full length. Strange, though: there were no fingernails. Maybe they would come later. I didn't really care.

I thought about Cazador. His name meant "hunter" – so had Jager's. One of them had hunted in the shadows, aware of the dark side of his work and careful not to cause too much damage. The other had hunted in public, protesting his innocence the entire time and wreaking untold harm.

Cazador had called me a monster. Until he had said it, I'd always agreed with that definition. Now I knew that a monster was not something that *could* prey on humans, but something that *did*. In that regard, I was a poor excuse for one. But Cazador fit the description to a T.

193

Then I thought about Ai Phuong. She'd had an eager, wild love of life, an elemental trust in the world and its ways that had gotten her killed. Was it smarter to be careful like me and survive? Or was it wiser to reach out and grab onto any adventure, heedless of the risk, and die too soon? I don't know.

Of all the vampires I'd met or heard of, Ai Phuong was the one I believed in the most. She had behaved like the archetypal night stalker of my imaginings. She'd killed humans with a lusty exuberance, remorseless and guiltless, but also without the self-righteous arrogance of so many bloodsuckers. She had lived on her own terms, simply and to the fullest.

Now that she was dead, I didn't really believe in vampires anymore.

Acknowledgments

Many sources have influenced this book, including works by these authors: Lee Child, James Clavell, Sue Grafton, Robert Heinlein, Gary Jennings, M.M. Kaye, John D. Macdonald, Stephenie Meyer, Robert B. Parker, Ann Rice, Joe Scalzi, Jerry Spinelli, Richard Stark, Andrew Vachss, Tom Wolfe, and John C. Wright.

Thanks to: Kaydee McKinney, for vetting the script; Terri Prizant, for cogent suggestions; my brother, George, for technical support; the Pasadena Central Library, for assistance and patience; Wikipedia.org, for its vast knowledge base; and the people at Amazon.com, for making it simple.

About the Author

Jim Hull received a degree in philosophy from the University of California at Santa Cruz, after which, like many a budding artist, he promptly became a ne'er-do-well, and for years he has worked in the performing arts. In the manner of some of his fellow vampires, Jim also pretends to be respectable – in his case, by writing and lecturing in the Los Angeles area.

You are cordially invited to post reviews of his books – including *Are Humans Obsolete?* – at amazon.com, kindle.amazon.com, and smashwords.com. Contact him with your comments or questions at: jimhull@jimhull.com

5582532R0

Made in the USA
Charleston, SC
06 July 2010